Hunting Season

ALSO BY ANDREA CAMILLERI

ANDREA CAMILLERI

Hunting Season

Translated by Stephen Sartarelli

MANTLE

First published 2014 by Penguin Books,
a member of Penguin Group (USA) Inc., New York

First published in the UK 2014 by Mantle
an imprint of Pan Macmillan, a division of Macmillan Publishers Limited
Pan Macmillan, 20 New Wharf Road, London N1 9RR
Basingstoke and Oxford
Associated companies throughout the world
www.panmacmillan.com

ISBN 978-1-4472-6591-7

Copyright © Sellerio Editore 1992
Translation copyright © Stephen Sartarelli 2014

Originally published in Italian 1992 as *La stagione della caccia* by Sellerio Editore, Palermo

The right of Andrea Camilleri to be identified as the
author of this work has been asserted by him in accordance
with the Copyright, Designs and Patents Act 1988.

1 3 5 7 9 8 6 4 2

A CIP catalogue record for this book is available from the British Library.

Printed and bound by CPI Group (UK) Ltd, Croydon, CR0 4YY

Hunting Season

One

The steam packet boat that delivered the post from Palermo, the *Re d'Italia* – which Sicilians stubbornly continued to call the *Franceschiello* out of a combination of habit, laziness, and homage to the Bourbon king who had instituted the service – moored, dead on time, at two o'clock in the afternoon of 1 January 1880, in the harbour of Vigàta.

Down a wobbly gangway of planks, promptly laid from dock to ship's side, the passengers from the hold came hurtling landward in a mayhem of cries, greetings, wails, bushels of fruit, sacks of potatoes, breadbaskets, bundles of chickens, and rocks of salt, while down a more dignified but even wobblier rigid boarding ladder came four cabin passengers duly honoured by Captain Cumella, who, watch in hand, was making it known that, come hell or high water, he and his boat were always punctual. Backtracking from the dock up to the deck, these passengers were: the postmaster of the Vigàta Post Office, Mr Carlo Colajanni, returning from Trapani, where he had gone with unflagging paternal solicitude to assist his only daughter Sarafina in giving birth for the eighth time; Mrs Clelia Tumminello, a woman of full-bodied beauty, afflicted, however, by an unknown ailment that compelled her to go once every two months to Castellammare for the required treatment – though the true benefit of these visits, according to gossips, came from the root extract her strapping young cousin, who hailed from those parts, was always ready to administer to her; and the commander of the garrison of Vigàta, Lieutenant Amedeo Baldovino, a Piedmontese from Cuneo, whose military hands buoyed Signora Clelia's haunches during her perilous descent down the boarding ladder.

Above these three, the top rungs remained vacant, because the fourth passenger, a young stranger not quite thirty years old in a checked suit and English cap, unre-markable in appearance, with a thin moustache and lean physique, stood with one foot on the deck and the other in midair, as if purposely trying, with that kick-like motion, to put a proper distance between himself and his fellow travellers.

He had, moreover, maintained that distance during the entire journey. Of few but courteous words when required, he became immediately tight-lipped the moment the others, in their curiosity, displayed any desire to know his name, surname, or profession.

Before descending the little rope ladder, the stranger waited for the trio before him to touch solid ground and dutifully exchange bows, handshakes, and tips of the hat. Then he made his move. But without haste, calm and poised, head turning first right, then left, to look at Vigàta's squat houses painted yellow, white, green, and blue. Suddenly there was not a soul left on the dock. The passengers and those waiting for them had all disappeared, swept away by an icy north wind. Reaching the bottom of the ladder, the stranger, who was holding only a small folding briefcase, turned and looked at Captain Cumella.

'About my trunk—' he began.

Captain Cumella interrupted him with a sweeping wave of the hand.

'Don't worry. I'll take care of it.'

The stranger needed only to cross two utterly lifeless streets to find himself in Vigàta's central piazza. Facing it were the church, the Nobles' Club, the three-storey palazzo of Baron Uccello, the two-storey house of Marquis Peluso, five trading shops for sulphur, almonds, and beans, the Sicilian Bank of Credit and Discount, and the Town Hall. Between the church and the club began the Corso, a narrow street like all the rest, though a bit less tortuous. Nor was there any sign of life in the piazza, except for a spotted dog blithely pissing at the foot of an odd statue without a pedestal next to the half-open door of the Nobles' Club. Between pale brown and grey in colour, and absurdly placed in a genuine wicker armchair, the monument represented a decrepit old man in a frock coat holding a walking stick in his crossed arms.

As the stranger resumed walking towards the Corso, the dog moved likewise, circling closely around the statue; then it stopped and raised its hind leg again, aiming straight at the frock coat, which touched the ground. Halfway across the square, the stranger froze in bewilderment. He had the troubling feeling that a pair of eyes were staring hard at him, though he couldn't tell where that menacing gaze was coming from. He took a few more steps, unconvinced that continuing in the open was the right thing to do; at that same moment, with the sort of slowness he had sometimes experienced in nightmares, the statue raised its right arm and waved its fingers weakly at him, clearly inviting him to come closer. Feeling his shirt suddenly stick to the sweat streaming down his back, the stranger stopped in front of the old man and bent down to see a face that looked like baked clay sculpted by long exposure to sunlight and frost, in whose deep wrinkles fly shit and pigeon droppings had formed a rough sort of paste; and under lashes encrusted with sand and sulphur dust, he discovered two knife-sharp, very living pupils. The old man contemplated the stranger for a few seconds in silence, began to shake all over, and opened his mouth as if to cry out in astonishment.

'*Madonna biniditta!*' he managed to rasp. Then he lowered his eyelids, repeating again to himself, this time almost in a tone of resignation: '*Madonna biniditta!*'

Polite and patient, with body bent forward, the stranger granted the old man all the time he needed to regain his breath and reopen his eyes.

'You are . . .' the old man began, but just as he was about to utter the stranger's name and surname, his memory suddenly slipped away, let go the rope dredged up with such effort from that black well of leaden recollections, got lost in a labyrinth of births and deaths, forgot events like wars and earthquakes, and seized fast upon something that had happened to the old man when he was barely four years old and his uncle's hunting dog had bitten him after he had poked it with a stick.

'You're a hunting dog,' the old man managed to conclude, shutting his eyelids tight, to let the other understand that he had no more intention of wasting his breath.

The stranger doffed his cap, bowed deeply to the man, who had turned back into a statue, and continued on his way.

Though not a day went by when he didn't steal some trifle or other, Sasà Mangione, a stevedore and porter in his free time, could not really be called a thief. And such was the conclusion reached by Portera the police inspector, after he had arrested Sasà some fifteen times.

'A thief because he pinches things from others?' the inspector had asked himself. 'If he had no money and made a little by selling what he stole, fine. But Sasà didn't need any money, since his wife was the maid of Commander Aguglia, a crazy ex-Garibaldian who said that all men are created almost equal and therefore paid his maid four times the going rate. What's more, Sasà did not sell what he took from others. Hadn't the inspector found Don Saverio Piscopo's magnifying glass, schoolmistress Pancucci's map of the world, and Dr Smecca's microscope safe and sound in Sasà's house? And so? There could only be one explanation: Sasà stole purely for the pleasure of depriving people of things. Sasà was not a thief, but a thieving magpie. And can one keep a bird in jail?'

One day Inspector Portera had summoned Sasà to the police station and told him the following:

'From now on, whenever somebody hires you to take something from one place to another, I want you to shout out, at the top of your lungs, every ten steps you take, where you picked it up, where you are taking it, and who it belongs to. If I catch you with so much as a blade of grass in your hand and you haven't cried out what I told you, I will send you to San Vito prison, where you'll end up feeding the worms.'

This was why, at four o'clock in the afternoon on that

New Year's Day, Sasà Mangione, staggering under the weight of an enormous trunk covered with shiny copper studs that made him sick to his stomach, knowing he couldn't unscrew them and take them home, trudged through the streets and piazzas of Vigàta, shouting:

'I got this trunk here from the *Franceschiello* when she arrived today . . . An' I'm takin' it to Mrs Concettina Adamo's boardinghouse . . . And it belongs to the stranger who arrived on the mail boat.'

Hearing these words, Mr Fede, the surveyor, who had been squirming in his effort to digest the half a roast kid he had eaten for lunch, leapt out of bed as though bitten by an animal, got dressed, and set off after the sound of Sasà's voice, which was now far away. The surveyor was known in town as a 'friend to strangers' for his extraordinary ability to approach outsiders who had just arrived and, with only a few questions, extract their whole life's story, which he would then recount to a captive audience at the club. He would have made a superb policeman, but had neither the head nor the heart of a cop. When he arrived at the boardinghouse out of breath, Sasà had just left, counting the money he'd been given.

'The stranger's not here; he's gone out for a walk,' said Signora Adamo before Mr Fede could open his mouth. 'I had the trunk taken up to his room. The stranger says it's not supposed to be opened for now. And he left me the money for Sasà. Satisfied, Mr Fede?'

'But did he let you know in advance he was coming?'

'Of course, last month he sent word with a sailor from the *Franceschiello*, who also brought four suitcases with him the last time she arrived.'

'So he's going to be here in Vigàta for a while?'

'He paid me in advance for fifteen days' room and board.'

'Do you know what his name is?'

'Of course. I've kept two letters that came for him. His name is Santo Alfonso de' Liguori.'

After combing the streets and alleyways around the harbour, Mr Fede caught up with the man as he was eyeing a palazzo with columns at the front. Although he had never seen him before, he knew him at once to be the stranger and approached him with the satisfaction of a pointer seeing his sense of smell confirmed.

'Hello. The name's Fede, surveyor by trade. Could I be of assistance to you in anything?'

'In nothing at all, thank you,' replied the stranger, touching his cap with two fingers.

'Beautiful building, isn't it?'

'Yes. It wasn't here before.'

'Before when?' the surveyor quickly replied, hoping to broaden that opening.

'Before,' the stranger repeated. And he walked away.

*

The moment he arrived in the piazza on his way back to the boardinghouse, the stranger felt the same uneasiness as the first time he had passed through. This time, however, he knew the reason and had no need to look for it. And indeed the old man had him in his sights again. So the stranger, too, stared back at him, straight in the eye, and began to draw near, with the measured step of someone approaching something dangerous. When he was in front of the old man, whose name he didn't know, he touched his cap with two fingers and said: 'Here I am.'

He was the first to be surprised. Why had those words come out of his mouth? What on earth was he saying or doing? And why?

The old man looked down and, as he had done that afternoon, muttered: '*Madonna biniditta!*'

'May I, sir?'

For the stranger – who was as taut as a violin string – the sound of another voice right beside him had the effect of a pistol shot. He took three quick steps back, ready to start running. The man who had spoken was tall and husky, dressed in black, completely bald, and looked to be about sixty. In his hand he held a blanket, which he then delicately wrapped around the old man's body. When he had finished, he turned and eyed the stranger.

'Need anything?'

'Goodbye,' was the stranger's reply.

*

An hour later, he couldn't stop thinking about what had happened. At last, no longer able to stand the torment, the stranger turned to Signora Adamo, who was serving him a dish of fried *calamaretti* and shrimps.

'Excuse me, signora, but do you know who that man in front of the Nobles' Club is?'

'There are so many idlers around there.'

'No, I was referring to a very old man who sits in a wicker chair.'

'Well, Mr Liquori—'

'Liguori.'

'—That's Marquis Peluso, Don Federico Maria *u vecchiu*, as they call him in town – "the elder", so as not to confuse him with his grandson, who has the same name.'

'So he would be the father of Marquis Don Filippo?'

'That's right.'

'But doesn't the old man have anyone to help him?'

'What do you mean? His manservant, Mimì, a tall man dressed in black without a hair on his head, carries him four times a day, in his chair, from his house to the club and back. He looks after him, brings him blankets if it's cold, removes his jacket when it's hot. And he's always keeping an eye on him from a window in Palazzo Peluso.'

'By "helping him" I meant, I dunno, changing his clothes, washing him . . . He looked utterly filthy to me.'

'The marquis's filth is his own business. It's nobody's fault. When Mimì tries to wash him even a little, the old man starts screaming so loud you'd think a pig was being slaughtered. One time, when he could still walk, he came here to eat with a friend and got some sauce on his hands. "Would you like to wash your hands, your excellency?" I asked him. "My dear," he replied, "for me, even rinsing my hands is a calamity." '

That evening, at the Nobles' Club, there was a general meeting to appoint the new members. The only person missing was Mr Fede.

'He must still be out hunting for strangers,' quipped Baron Uccello.

Marquis Peluso requested permission to speak. 'Before we begin considering names,' he said, 'I have a serious proposal to make. And that is, that the Nobles' Club should no longer be called that.'

'Why not?' asked Lieutenant Amedeo Baldovino.

'Because there are only two nobles left here, me and Baron Uccello. Everyone else — and far be it from me to offend anyone — hasn't got the slightest connection to the nobility. Perhaps we should call our club the "Club of Two Nobles and their Relatives". The whole thing makes me laugh.'

'The marquis is right!' enthusiastically replied the ex-Garibaldino Aguglia, the commander who was convinced that all men were almost equal. 'Let's call it the Garibaldi Club.'

They began, in silence, to contemplate the proposal. Then Dr Smecca asked to speak.

'I don't agree with Marquis Peluso,' he said. 'Everyone should know that I speak only for myself, of course. I am not noble but, personally, I rather like being a member of the Nobles' Club, whereas I couldn't care less about belonging to some common Garibaldi Club.'

As all present were applauding Dr Smecca, Fede the surveyor came in. The hall suddenly grew silent again.

'Nothing.'

'Weren't you able to talk to him?' asked Baldovino, who, after just two years in the town, had become more Vigatese than the Vigatese.

'Oh, I talked to him, all right. And he's polite, of course, but prickly and standoffish.'

'Yes, he certainly is standoffish,' the lieutenant seconded him. 'During the entire journey here, neither Mr Colajanni nor Signora Clelia could extract a single tidbit of information from him.'

'Why,' said Colajanni, slightly piqued, 'didn't you try to extract anything yourself?'

'I certainly did,' said Baldovino, smiling.

'But I did find out one thing,' the surveyor cut in, pausing slyly after making this statement. 'His name.'

'What is it?' they all asked in chorus.

'His name is Santo Alfonso de' Liguori.'

Father Macaluso, who according to his custom was sitting off to the side, sulking and reading the newspaper, suddenly lit up like a match. 'What the hell did you say?'

'The owner of the boardinghouse told me that was his name.'

'The owner of the boardinghouse was pulling your leg. That's the name of a saint!'

'Isn't that what I said? His name's Santo!'

'You nitwit! Alfonso de' Liguori is a saint, not someone whose first name is Santo!'

'I beg your pardon, Father Macaluso,' Baron Uccello calmly intervened, 'but is it somehow forbidden that someone should have Santo as his first name, Alfonso as his middle name, and de' Liguori as his surname?'

'It's not forbidden, but it sounds like humbug to me.'

'And did you find out how long he'll be staying in Vigàta?' Colajanni the postmaster asked.

'A fortnight. Which means I'll have all the time I need to find out how many hairs he's got on his arse.'

In the end, however, he proved unable to count these hairs – to continue the metaphor – for it was the stranger himself who decided at a certain point to let everyone know who he was and what he had come to do in Vigàta.

Having hired a horse and cabriolet, the stranger began going back and forth to Montelusa, where the administrative offices were. Here he was seen entering the Royal Prefecture, the Royal Commissariat of Police, the Royal

Tax Office, and many other no less royal venues. But the purpose of this grand tour remained unknown. One evening Santo Alfonso was seen walking around the harbour and speaking in a low voice to Bastiano Taormina, a man with whom it was considered unwise to break bread and whom it was better not to meet at night.

Fede the surveyor, who had witnessed the meeting from a distance, was unable to sleep for the rest of the night, so keenly was his curiosity eating him alive. Very early the next morning, shaking inside like a jelly, he paid a visit to Bastiano Taormina's greengrocer's shop.

'And a very good morning to you, Don Bastiano!' he greeted the greengrocer, leaning against the door jamb in a pose that looked nonchalant but was in fact dictated by the need to lean against something. Taormina, who was unloading a crate of peas, didn't respond.

'May I come in?'

'Go ahead.'

Now that he had to say something, the surveyor felt his mouth go all dry.

'I have a question, just one, and then I'll leave you to your work. Who is Santo Alfonso de' Liguori?'

The other stared back at him with bovine eyes. 'A saint. My mother prays to him.'

'No, I'm sorry, I didn't make myself clear. Who is the stranger?'

'A man,' said Taormina, his eyes darkening.

Fede did not insist, realizing that one question more might prove fatal.

But the surveyor did manage nevertheless to gain satisfaction.

'I know the whole story!' he cried triumphantly two days later to his friends and the club. 'Mr de' Liguori has bought the house that used to belong to Taormina's brother, Jano, who died at sea. It's right on the Corso, near my place, and has a shop downstairs and a flat above. The masons and carpenters start work tomorrow.'

'Why has he come to Vigàta?'

'I know that too,' said the surveyor, puffing up with pride like a peacock. 'He's going to open a pharmacy.'

Thus nobody was curious when, the next few times the *Franceschiello* came into the harbour, Sasà Mangione unloaded huge trunks stuffed so full they risked giving him a hernia with every step he took; and nobody was curious when a box full of glass tubes and bottles and flasks in previously unseen forms arrived at the post office; and nobody was curious when de' Liguori the pharmacist spent the morning combing the countryside looking for and gathering certain kinds of grasses and flowers. These things were all part of his profession.

'He's thought everything out very carefully,' said Fede the surveyor. 'On the ground floor there's the pharmacy, behind which there's a great big room full of counters with glass instruments on them. There are also two big containers full of water and a little oven for drying plants. There's also a door in this back room which gives onto the street, so that if the pharmacist wants to come and go when the shop is closed, he doesn't have to open the front door; and there's a broad wooden staircase that leads to the flat upstairs, where there's a living and dining room, the bedroom, the kitchen, and a toilet.'

'What is the bed like?'

'Small.'

'A sign he doesn't want to settle down,' said Mr Colajanni, who had two marriageable daughters.

'You're telling us things that anyone can see with his own eyes,' Baron Uccello interrupted, 'but you still can't tell us who Santo Alfonso de' Liguori is nor why he got it in his head to set up a pharmacy in Vigàta.'

'That is the question,' the surveyor said, pensively.

'Tomorrow afternoon they're going to open a pharmacy in town,' Mimì said as he was carrying his master, chair and all, from the palazzo to the club. He often told him of the goings-on about town, such as, 'Pippineddu the mason fell from a ladder and broke his leg,' or 'Mrs Balistreri gave birth to a baby daughter,' and he would say these things just to amuse him and help the time pass, knowing he would never reply. But as he was covering him with the blanket, since it was late February and frosty, the old man made as if to speak. 'No,' he said with such effort that he began to sweat, despite the cold. 'No, Mimì. Tomorrow the hunting season opens.'

'What are you saying, sir? It's a pharmacy that's opening, and the pharmacist is that stranger gentleman who greets you every time he passes by.'

'No, Mimì, tomorrow the hunting season opens. And I don't want to get shot.'

'But what are you afraid of, sir? What, are you a quail or something?'

Mimì was dumbfounded. The marquis had not spoken so much in years.

The old man bobbed his head forward, as if to say yes. 'But I *am* a quail, Mimì; it is just as you say.'

He took a long, deep breath, exhausted from all the words he was saying.

'And remember one thing, Mimì. I don't want to get shot. I would sooner kill myself.'

Mimì paid no mind. His master had not been quite right in the head for some time.

'Shall I go and get a basin, warm some water, and wash your hands?'

By way of reply, the old man's terrified scream shook the windowpanes on the door of the club.

The bomb went off half an hour after the pharmacy was inaugurated.

'Something's not right,' said Fede the surveyor, arriving out of breath.

'Not a bloody thing's right for me,' said Baron Uccello, who was losing game after game.

'The pharmacist hired Fillicò, the carriage painter, to make his sign. Fillicò made it picture-perfect and just now hung it over the door. You know what it says?'

'"Pharmacy",' said Lieutenant Baldovino.

'Right, but just below, instead of the proprietor's name, Santo Alfonso de' Liguori, there's a different name: Alfonso La Matina.'

'Pharmacy, Alfonso La Matina,' the lieutenant summarized.

'But if his name is Alfonso La Matina, why did he say it was Santo Alfonso de' Liguori?' asked Baron Uccello, asking the question that was in everybody's mind.

'*Madonna biniditta!*' Marquis Peluso exclaimed, lost in thought. '*Madonna biniditta!*' he repeated, unaware he was using the same expression his father had used upon seeing the stranger. He shot to his feet, grabbed his coat and hat, and ran out of the club.

He returned half an hour later, appearing at once pleased and unconvinced.

'I talked to him,' he said. 'You know who he is? He's Fofò, Santo La Matina's son. Do you remember Santo?'

'Of course I remember him,' said Baron Uccello after a

moment's pause. 'He was that farmhand of your father's, who had a magical garden in a secret place.'

'That's the one,' said the marquis.

'A magical garden?' said Lieutenant Baldovino, sceptically.

'Oh yes, Lieutenant, and it was magical indeed,' the marquis explained. 'I saw it myself. A little patch of earth with all of God's bounty in it. And, as a matter of fact, those vegetables, herbs, and fruits could cure anything.'

'Are you pulling my leg?'

'No. And if you don't believe me, you can ask anyone who still remembers it, like Baron Uccello, here present. Then, one day some twenty years ago, Santo and his son Fofò disappeared. Or rather, Fofò alone disappeared; he was about ten years old at the time. Santo was found a foot underground with his throat slashed. His killers had burned down his garden and scattered salt over it.'

'Were the culprits ever found?'

'Never. And that is precisely why Fofò La Matina, when he came here to open his pharmacy, used a different name. He was afraid that some of his father's killers might still be in town.'

'And how does he know now they're not still around?'

'Because, apart from buying a house, he talked to Bastiano Taormina. And Bastiano told him everything he needed to know. But the pharmacist didn't tell me what Bastiano said. He only told me how that night, four masked men came for them and wanted to kill him, too. But Fofò hid behind a big bush with the bag of money his father had managed to hand him just before the killers entered the house. When the masked men left, Fofò escaped, taking eight days to get to Palermo, where he went to a cousin of his father's who was a priest and recognized him. You can imagine the rest. But I can tell you one thing: if Fofò has a quarter of his father's talent, that pharmacy is going to make him rich.'

The latest bit of news concerning the pharmacist was a strictly private matter, which, nevertheless, as always happened in Vigàta, immediately became public. To wit: Signora Clelia had not been able to stomach something that happened on her way home from Palermo on the *Franceschiello*. At one point during the journey, as everyone was eating, Captain Cumella had come out and said that thirty years earlier, at the exact spot at which they found themselves, a three-masted Austrian ship had sunk for no apparent reason with all her passengers and crew. Upon hearing this, Signora Clelia decided to have an attack. She stiffened and began shaking her head to the left and right, moaning and rolling her eyes backwards. It was a manoeuvre she always pulled off rather well, having practised it whenever something didn't go her way since the age of eight. The three men with her, Captain Cumella, Mr Colajanni, and Lieutenant Baldovino, rushed to her aid without a moment's hesitation, with Captain Cumella opening her mouth and making her drink some water, Mr Colajanni fanning her with his napkin, and Lieutenant Baldovino unlacing her bodice with his dextrous hands. The only one who did not budge was the person for whom the entire drama was being performed: the stranger, now identified as Fofò La Matina the pharmacist, who stood the whole time to one side, smoothing his moustache. And now Signora Clelia wished to avenge herself for his indifference. One day, when she learned from her maid, Cicca, that Dr Smecca was ill, she decided she urgently needed to see a doctor.

'But where are you going to go, if Smecca is unavailable? Would you like me to accompany you to Girgenti?' asked her husband, unaware that the horns on his head were so tall that they could have been used as lighthouses.

'There's no need. I'll go and see the new pharmacist. I have the impression he's very good.'

She washed herself from head to toe, using an entire jug of water, doused herself in Coty perfume, bedizened herself in black Brussels-lace knickers and bra (an already tested tool able to turn a bent blade of grass into rock-hard pitch-pine), powdered her nose, dolled herself up, and went to the pharmacy.

'What do you want?' the pharmacist asked.

You, Signora Clelia wanted to reply, but instead she said: 'I want you to examine me.'

'I am not a doctor, signora.'

'I know. But I am told you are talented. And I need to be examined so badly that you cannot even imagine it.'

'I take no responsibility,' said the pharmacist. Then he turned towards a boy he had hired as his assistant. 'If anyone comes,' he said, 'tell them I'll be back in five minutes.'

'Do you think five minutes will be enough?' asked Signora Clelia, batting her eyelashes.

The pharmacist invited her to follow him up the wooden staircase to the living and dining room, sat her down, and enquired as to what was ailing her. As she was speaking, and without Fofò's having asked, Signora Clelia quickly stripped down to her black Brussels lace, looking from time to time towards the bedroom. The pharmacist listened to her, dead serious.

'Please get dressed, signora, and go back downstairs,' he said. 'In the meantime I'll prepare something for you.'

Signora Clelia later recounted the whole episode, blow by blow, to her bosom friend and confidante, Mrs Colajanni, a churchgoing woman who spent her life talking and gossiping about others. That same evening, Colajanni the postmaster told the club about it. The opinions and comments varied greatly.

'The pharmacist doesn't have a cock,' was the most categorical.

'The pharmacist doesn't like Signora Clelia,' was the most plausible.

'The pharmacist is a true gentleman who will not go with other men's wives,' was the most amicable.

'The pharmacist is an idiot,' was the most drastic.

On the morning of the last day in February, Mimì opened his master's bedroom door, intending to dress him, carry him out on his chair, and set him down outside the club. The bed was unmade but the marquis was not in it. The old man was capable, in moments of need, of taking two or three steps by himself. But there was no sign of him in the toilet, either. Mimì thought that his master had perhaps needed something during the night and summoned his family for help, and so he went and quietly opened the doors to the bedrooms of Don Filippo and his wife, and of Marchesina 'Ntontò and Marchesino Rico. They were all fast asleep. Worried, he ran down to the kitchen, where Peppinella the maid was already at work. But she, too, knew nothing. Alarmed, Peppinella also began looking for the old marquis. They searched and searched again, from attic to cellar to storehouse and stables, but of Don Federico there wasn't a trace.

'I'm going to tell Don Filippo,' said Mimì.

'Look here,' Peppinella called out, stopping him. Leading from the old man's room was an almost invisible trail, interrupted here and there, of grains of sand, sulphur dust, and dried pigeon droppings. Mimì followed it to the end of the broad stone staircase and noticed that the front door was open. Going out into the courtyard, he saw that the great entrance to the palazzo was also half open. Running frantically, he combed the entire town all the way to the harbour in less than fifteen minutes, asking everyone he ran into if by any chance they had seen an old man fitting such-and-such a description. But nobody was of any help. And so he started running down the beach, along the water's edge, the sea soaking his shoes and trousers. Then, in the distance, he saw a black object that the waves were turning over and over. He approached, growing weak in the knees. It was his master. He went into the water, dragged the marquis to the shore, and went back into town to look for Dr Smecca. But the doctor, who was running a very high fever, couldn't get out of bed.

'Call the pharmacist,' the doctor suggested.

Fofò La Matina didn't waste a second. A moment later, he was racing behind Mimì, who was running like a hare. When they reached their destination, they found Inspector Portera, summoned by a passing fisherman.

'It's no use,' said the inspector. 'He's been dead for a few hours. Killed himself.'

'But he hadn't walked for years!' said the pharmacist.

'Well, this time he walked just fine. At some point he fell, dropped his cane, and continued on his hands and knees. Then he couldn't go any further that way, either, and so he started dragging himself along.'

'How do you know these things? Who told you?' said Mimì.

'The sand told me, Mimì,' said Portera. 'Have a look for yourself. It's all written in the sand. The marquis was determined to kill himself. But I don't think he drowned.'

Mimì walked away, retracing his master's last efforts in reverse. The inspector was right.

'So how did he die then?' asked the pharmacist.

'Heart failure. He was too old and too tired, and the water was too cold.'

His son, the marquis, arrived half dressed, having been informed by one of the inspector's men.

'Poor Papà! What a terrible way for him to die,' he said upon seeing the old man's body, scrubbed utterly clean by the sea. 'It's as if he died washing himself.'

Two

Federico Maria Santo was the twenty-two-year-old heir to the line of Marquis Peluso di Torre Venerina. Practically speaking, Federico Maria was not so much an offspring of the legitimate union of Don Filippo with Donna Matilde Barletta-Capodirù as a product, a fruit, of the enchanted garden of the legendary Santo La Matina, quite like the pears that induced rivers of piss, the peaches that caused enormous turds, the cicely that cured asthma, and the bitter almonds that overcame malaria once and for all.

After conceiving their eldest daughter Antonietta, known to all as 'Ntontò, with the listless performance of her husband the marquis, and bringing her happily into the world to the joy of family, friends, and relatives (a joy shared only for the sake of appearances and personal honour by the father, who would have preferred a son), Donna Matilde believed that her obligations as woman and mother had been fulfilled. Great, therefore, was her surprise when, the first night back in her bed, just after putting out the lamp, her husband came looking for her and thereafter persisted in trying to attain his goal, despite the fact that she complained of a wandering pain that would migrate, on a whim, sometimes towards her stomach, sometimes towards her head.

One night the marchesa, already mauled by three endless penetrations about an hour apart, had just drifted off to sleep on her side when, at the toll of the bell calling worshippers to morning Mass, she felt her husband's hands grab her yet again. And in the twinkling of an eye she found herself facedown with her legs spread. It was, for the marchesa, the most comfortable position, one which allowed her to doze for some ten minutes while her spouse laboured and sweated behind her. This time, however, the marchesa remained awake and, indeed, spoke out. The upshot was that at the sound of her voice her husband was paralysed in astonishment, given that, according to the teachings of the late Father Carnazza, who had joined them in holy matrimony, relations between man and wife must take place in strict silence – with the only allowance being made for the utterance, on the woman's part, of a short prayer suited for the occasion, but in a soft voice, as though sighing.

'Why?' Donna Matilde asked bluntly, raising her cheek slightly from the pillow.

'Why what?' the marquis asked back, panting but continuing to impale her firmly.

'Why are you doing what you're doing?'

A bull, when asked this sort of question, would have become confused and let everything drop. But the marquis was made of iron ore.

'Because I want you to give me a son,' he said and resumed riding her.

The attempt to impregnate the marchesa went on for almost two years, and Donna Matilde began seriously considering retiring to the convent of Santa Maria di Cupertino, lost in the Madonie Mountains, where it was said that no man had ever set foot over the threshold.

'Of course not, because the men come and go through the windows,' quipped Baron Uccello, an unbeliever and, on this occasion, an important adviser to the marquis concerning the manner most suitable for conceiving the heir to the house of Peluso di Torre Venerina.

'Have you tried the position the Germans call "the dancing bear"?'

'Yes. Nothing.'

'How about the one the Arabs call "the serpentine"?'

'That too. All to no avail. You see, my friend, I am convinced that success in this matter has nothing whatsoever to do with the position or the day or the sun or the moon. There has to be another reason. Nor can it be a case of what Dr Smecca calls *impotentia generandi*, since I've already had a daughter.'

At these words Baron Uccello had a sudden flash, a suspicion that burst inside him like a shot in the silence of the night. He quickly buried its echo in the deepest recesses of his consciousness, but a vivid twinkle in his eyes sufficed to give him away. The marquis had already read the thought and its implications in his gaze as clearly as if it had been printed black on white.

'If you ever get that look in your eyes again – and I know what it means,' said the marquis in a single breath, 'I'll shoot you on the spot. My wife is a virtuous woman. And I don't even have any brothers.'

In asserting he was an only son, Don Filippo was alluding to the well-known story of Baron Ardigò, who, unable to conceive a son, and having ascertained that it was he, and not the baroness, who was sterile, had resorted to the 'second barrel' – as hunters called it – that is, his younger brother, who rose to the task quite willingly and impregnated his pretty sister-in-law, whom he had long coveted, at the first go. 'Actually, there's another concern that gives me no rest,' the marquis resumed, the offence forgotten. 'And it's this: what if, after all this effort, my wife ends up suckling another girl?'

'Why, don't you follow the Sciabarrà method?' the baron asked in astonishment.

'No. What's that?'

'The Sciabarrà method—'

'Is he a doctor?'

'A doctor? Sciabarrà? No, he's the municipal accountant. But he has eight sons with cocks between their legs. Isn't that enough? At any rate, I got my two boys using his method. So, to be sure to have a son, you have to fast for an entire day, walk twelve miles in the evening, and then have sexual relations immediately afterwards.'

The marquis did not seem very enthusiastic about the idea.

'But is it certain?'

'It's guaranteed. Look at Totò Cumbo. After three girls, he practised the Sciabarrà method and had a son.'

After strict application of the method for one month, the marquis fainted in the town square. He suddenly collapsed when racing back to his palazzo after his daily twelve miles, trousers and shoes covered with mud because the heavens had opened the floodgates that day. Unable to explain the marquis's sudden deterioration, Dr Smecca prescribed tonic treatments and a month in bed. Donna Matilde immediately took advantage of this, changing room and bed with the excuse of not wanting to disturb her husband, and thus was able finally to shut her eyes as well as other parts of her body.

'I'm wasting time,' Don Filippo said to his friend Uccello, who had come to see him. 'I feel like a tethered hunter, watching the hare run away.'

The baron smiled and gave him a mysterious look. 'Don't despair,' he said. 'I have a wonderful idea. Trust me.'

Three days later Baron Uccello paid him a visit with a parcel under his arm, eyes twinkling with contentment. After making sure no one would disturb them, he set about opening it delicately. Out came a cucumber the length of a forearm and firm, clearly the product of hybridization, since grafted at one end were two peaches as big as the knobs on a bedstead. The marquis looked dumbfounded at the enormous vegetable phallus.

'I paid a call on Santo La Matina. I described your situation. He didn't want to hear about it, said it's wrong to go against nature. I threw myself at his feet, and in the end he was moved to pity. And here's the solution.'

The marquis felt more and more confused.

'Am I supposed to use that thing? It's not going to be easy to convince my wife.'

'What kind of ideas are you getting in your head? You're supposed to gobble it up. Without removing the skin, you are to cut it into slices and soak them in a mug of red wine. Then you must eat the cucumber and peaches at the crack of dawn on the first day of the second quarter of the moon, which will be in a week's time. Do you follow?'

'Will that be enough?'

'Let me finish.'

He slipped his hand back into the parcel and pulled

out a tiny envelope, which he opened with great care. Inside were two seeds that looked like they came from a watermelon, blackish and dried up.

'Now, you are to swallow these seeds with a bit of water before having relations.'

'And you think it will work?'

'It's guaranteed to work.'

'But you also said the Sciabarrà method was guaranteed.'

'Well, you can forget about that now.'

It worked. Exactly nine months later, Federico Maria Santo Peluso di Torre Venerina came into the world to the tearful joy of the marquis and the genuine delight of Donna Matilde, who knew the nightmare of her nightly persecution was over. The third name given the newborn, Santo, was clearly a token of thanks from the marquis to La Matina for the pharmacist's horticultural wizardry. Equally clear was the fact that the baby, with his melon-like head, potato nose, and watermelon-seed eyes, still belonged to the vegetable kingdom.

As he grew up, Federico Maria Santo, for simplicity's sake, came to be called Rico by the rest of the family, but the children he played with quickly renamed him Ricò. The accent on the last syllable was not a form of endearment, but rather a judgement of his character. Since *ricò* meant none other than ricotta cheese – '*A ricò! Cu a voli a ricò!*' the street vendor would cry out in the early morning with his cart full of cheese baskets – that accent implied that the matter inside Federico Maria's skull, as well as the boy's bearing, consisted of fresh, quivering ricotta. Rico was thus a bit sweet in the head, his thoughts never coming out seasoned with the salt that would seem to be a feature of human brain function, and this was perhaps why he enjoyed a perpetually serene temperament and never took offence at anything. Unable to string more than two words together in a sentence, he often burst into a laughter that had nothing human about it, but sounded exactly like the bleating of a goat.

On the evening of 30 June 1880, as they were all eating supper, Rico announced to the family that he didn't want any celebrations for the following day, his twenty-second birthday. He was going to get up very early in the morning, take a horse, and meet Bonocore the manager at the edge of the Citronella woods, which he said were a sort of inexhaustible mine of mushrooms. Rico was, in fact, a glutton for raw mushrooms. He had even had some leather bags expressly made with several pouches in which he kept special knives, a little rake, a sickle, a hook, a small box of salt, and a bottle of vinegar. Whenever he found mushrooms, he would eat them on the spot. He never brought them home; he claimed they lost their flavour that way.

'You're all worked up over the mushrooms in the Citronella,' said Don Filippo, 'when there are far more in the Zàgara woods.'

'Yes, but less tasty.'

He left the next morning at dawn, shotgun on his shoulder. The double barrels were just for show; Rico would never have been able to use it against another living being. The sight of a sparrow with a grain of wheat in its beak, a rabbit scampering into the undergrowth, an ant dragging a piece of straw filled him with a strange happiness, and a kind of music began to play inside him, growing louder and louder until he burst out in a colossal bleat.

When, after a three-hour ride, he arrived at the clearing in front of Bonocore's house, Carmelina came running up to him, breathless. She was his secret. It wasn't at all true that the mushrooms in the Citronella woods were more flavourful than the others. But at the manager's house lived Carmelina, the only creature, he was sure, who could understand him deep down inside. Their love had begun a year earlier and still endured, while growing in intensity. For a year now, Rico had been wondering what had first attracted Carmelina to him, what was the origin of the miracle he was living. He had been speaking – he confusedly remembered as he embraced Carmelina and kissed her – with the manager, who had told him something that made him laugh; and, upon hearing his laugh, Carmelina, who was at the edge of the clearing, had suddenly turned around and started walking slowly towards him without taking her eyes off him. Yes, that was how it had all begun: with his laughing. He kissed Carmelina again and, feeling he could not hold out much longer, he called out the manager's name, to see if he was around. There was no reply; the coast was clear. And so, almost by force, he dragged her into the thatched hut, took off his clothes, and lay down on the ground, naked. With patience and devotion, Carmelina began to lick him. A few moments later, realizing he was about to explode like a wild cucumber and scatter his seed all around, Carmelina turned her back to him and waited to feel the weight of her man on her body.

As soon as he entered the woods, still sweaty from love-making, Rico began to recite the litany: *Clavaria pistillaria, Elvella mitrata, Morchella esculenta, Amanita caesarea* . . . These were the scientific names of the mushrooms he had learned by heart by studying over and over the plates in Marsigli's *De generatione fungorum*, a 1714 book he had bought from a friend for a small fortune. The litany was an enhancement, an evocative foretaste of the real pleasure of the mushroom he would soon savour. Once he was inside and had a look around, he came to an abrupt halt. In the middle of a dense thicket of brambles, he thought he saw the pale, bald head of an infant a few months old with its eyes torn out. The rest of the little body was not visible. Rico shuddered in fear, and was immediately tempted to run away. But he summoned his courage and began to draw near, back bent, one slow step at a time, hunching over as if to avoid a blow. When he was at arm's length and could see more clearly, he sighed in relief and let out a deafening bleat: what he had seen was an enormous mushroom, by far the biggest he had ever seen. Overcome with excitement, he reached down, armed with the little sickle, paying no mind to the prickles shredding his palm and the back of his hand.

Carmelina became worried when Rico was late returning. Night was falling, and she knew that he didn't like to walk at night. Even his horse, tied to a tree trunk, was getting restless. No longer able to contain her anxiety, Carmelina started running towards the woods. She only had to go in a short way: Rico was leaning against a tree, eyes closed, spittle dripping out of his mouth, not responding to the sound of her voice desperately calling him. And it was those cries that made the manager come running.

'Blood of Christ!' Bonocore cursed and, perhaps to relieve himself of the fright he felt at the sight of Rico, who looked already dead, he dealt the howling Carmelina a powerful kick. But the nanny goat didn't budge an inch.

For two hours Donna Matilde had been wailing like Mary at the foot of the cross, hopping around next to the bed on which Rico lay dying.

'They killed him! They shot my son!'

In vain 'Ntontò tried to stop her, in vain she told her it had not been a murder, that it had only been a misfortune. To no avail. At most, Donna Matilde would utter a variant, in a voice so shrill that the horses in the stables answered back.

'They cut him down with guns!'

The marquis looked glumly on, motionless as a statue, as Dr Smecca and the pharmacist La Matina, summoned for consultation, busied themselves with the moribund Rico, but at a certain point he sprang to his feet from the little sofa on which he had been sitting beside his friend Uccello, and, in a very calm tone that contrasted with the violence with which he had stood up, called his wife.

'Come here, you silly goose.'

The woman approached, trembling all over.

'Either you pipe down,' he continued, 'or I'm going to give you a kicking.'

Donna Matilde withdrew to a corner, whimpering softly.

'You have to forgive her, poor woman,' said Baron Uccello, adding, at precisely the wrong moment: 'Just think of all she had to put up with to conceive him.'

The marquis looked at him thoughtfully. 'Baron, would you do me a most welcome favour?'

'By all means,' said the other, leaping to his feet.

'Would you please get the hell out of here?'

Now the Baron Uccello was a good, kind man, but he

also had a knack for kicking up a row in any circumstance – even such as the present one, in front of a dying man.

'No one has ever told me to get the hell out of anywhere, you know.'

'Well, now you know what it's like.'

They were interrupted by Fofò La Matina.

'Could I have your attention, please?' He looked over at Dr Smecca, who was on the other side of the bed, and continued: 'The doctor is right. It is a clear case of mushroom poisoning. Don Rico must have mistaken an *Amanita virosa*, which is lethal and grows in abundance in those parts, with *Agaricus silvaticus*, which is edible. A tragic mistake.'

Donna Matilde's cry startled them all, including Rico, who opened his eyes for a moment then closed them again.

'No! My son was a god of mushrooms! He would never have made a mistake! He was shot! With pistols!'

Federico Maria Santo Peluso di Torre Venerina, heir to the title, did not make it to midnight. He breathed his last at 11:59, practically choking on the Viaticum the choleric Father Macaluso had forced into his mouth, leaving Rico no longer able to swallow with the wafer stuck between his palate and throat. But he was going to die one way or another.

The day after the funeral, the marquis disappeared after informing Baron Uccello:

'My good friend, I'm in need of some distraction, to cheer myself up. I'm going to go and spend some time on my estate. I don't enjoy sitting down at table with my family any more.'

'Have they done something to upset you?'

'Nothing at all. You see, my friend, when my father threw himself into the sea for reasons known only to him—'

'What do you mean, for reasons known only to him? He was ninety years old, had been glued to a chair for ten, depending on others – if I may say so – to wipe his arse . . .'

'So what? My father would have enjoyed life anyway, to the last drop, even with his arms and legs cut off and stuck inside a pot of parsley. Forget about it. No, I'm not going back home, and I'll tell you why. When my father killed himself, I put on a black tie and a black armband a foot wide. Since Rico died, we're all dressed in black and are in deep mourning. Even the servants wear black. Yesterday evening, at the dinner table, we looked like a flock of crows being served by crows. I need a change of scene for a little while, my friend.'

The marquis made a first, brief stop at Bonocore's house.

'I want you to tell me, in minute detail, exactly what happened.'

'Your excellency must know that on that same accursed

day I had to go to Sant'Agata to buy seeds. I returned at nightfall, but didn't know that your son had come here. I only realized it when I saw his horse tied to a tree. And as I was saddling my she-mule I heard Carmelina—'

'Who is Carmelina?'

'That goat who's looking at us over there. She was screaming like hell, an' I thought she got lost in the woods or some animal'd bit her. So I ran out to look for her and found 'er next to your son. It looked like Don Rico'd managed to drag himself out of the wood and crawl towards my house, but 'e didn't quite make it. 'E was leaning against a tree and 'd thrown up and shat 'is pants, with all due respect. So I picked 'im up an' put 'im on 'is 'orse and brought 'im into town. I lost some time when the goat kept following after me, acting like she was crazy, and I had to turn back and lock 'er in the thatched hut.'

He paused.

''Cause your excellency should know that Carmelina . . .' He stopped.

'. . . that Carmelina and Don Rico were in love.'

'Oh, really?'

'Yes.'

Silence fell. The marquis then cut a slice of bread from the loaf he had in his haversack and walked up to Carmelina. The animal stood still, waiting until the marquis was three steps away before preparing to sidestep.

'There's a good girl,' said Don Filippo, crouching and

tossing the bread to the goat. 'I only wanted to thank you for bringing a little happiness to my son.'

He stood up, returned to Bonocore, took his wallet out of his jacket, extracted some notes, and held them out. Bonocore felt faint; he had never seen so much money.

'Make her a nice house – for Carmelina, that is. One with a roof. And buy the best food you can for her.'

'For the goat?!'

'No, not "for the goat", as you put it. No. For Carmelina, my son's beloved.'

Bonocore felt like laughing, but he held himself back when he saw the look in his master's eyes.

'And if, when I come back, I find you haven't done what I asked, I'll give you such a thrashing I'll leave you for dead in a deep valley somewhere.'

Bonocore realized it was no time for joking.

'I swear on my life,' he said, putting his right hand over his heart. 'She'll be treated like a queen.'

The marquis's second, much longer stop was at the cottage of Natale Pirrotta, the field watcher for Le Zubbie, his twenty-thousand-hectare vineyard. The cottage sat on a hill covered with Saracen olive trees, and from some of its windows one could see the distant line of the sea. It also displayed a recently added room on top, whitewashed on the outside and equipped with a cupboard for his needs. Pirrotta had built it two years earlier for Don Filippo, after they had come to an agreement. The field watcher was a burly man who had long been married to a hard-working woman with a generous heart who had only one great defect: she couldn't bear children. This problem of hers had won her the sympathy of the marquis, who, at the time, was trying to have a son. When the field watcher's wife died falling from the roof, where she had climbed to fix a gutter, Natale, after the required period of mourning, decided to find another woman. Dr Smecca, who was sort of a spiritual father to Pirrotta, advised him to marry Trisina, the beautiful eighteen-year-old daughter of a former maid of his. When Pirrotta remarked that there would be an age difference of a good thirty years between husband and wife, the doctor replied that this was exactly what was needed for Natale finally to have a son: firm, young flesh, fertile ground for tired seed.

'And what if she won't have me? What if, I dunno, she thinks I'm too old?'

'Oh, she'll have you, she'll have you, don't you worry about that. I'm going to talk to her mother tomorrow.'

The first night he spent with his new bride in the cottage at Le Zubbie, Pirrotta was able to touch with his hand, so to speak, the fact that Dr Smecca had already dipped his bread in Trisina. But he played dumb, deciding to consider the woman a necessary tool for having a child, the way a bucket is needed to draw water from a well or a hoe is needed to break up the soil. Three years later, however, there were still no children. One evening Pirrotta went upstairs to the room where he slept with Trisina in their double bed, and he separated the frames, planks, and mattresses.

'I don't need you any more,' he said to Trisina, showing her the now twin beds. 'You can go back to fucking the doctor.'

One day when they were on the trail of a hare, Pirrotta spoke about the matter with his master.

'But do you really not care if Smecca fucks her?' asked the marquis.

'Him or someone else, it's all the same to me.'

'What if it was me?'

'I'd be honoured,' said the field watcher.

They made an agreement, and Pirrotta built the extra room so that Don Filippo, when he came to see Trisina, could stay at his convenience.

Worn out from the ride from Citronella to Le Zubbie, the marquis had just finished washing, and had not yet changed his clothes, when he heard the field watcher call to him. He went to the window. Pirrotta was standing beside his saddled she-mule in the little clearing by the well.

'I'm going to the livestock fair at Mascalucia. I'll be away for three days and three nights. If you need anything, ask Trisina. With your blessing, sir.'

He mounted his mule and left. Pirrotta was keen to

save face even when they were alone. After a short while the marquis saw Trisina go to the well, remove her bodice, and begin washing herself. He lay down on the bed, closed his eyes for a spell, then reopened them when he heard a noise. Trisina, completely naked, tits pointing proudly at him, was standing in the doorway, smiling.

When Don Filippo Peluso arrived at the front door of his palazzo after being away for eight days (having sent Pirrotta on a few other errands), the first thing he heard was the shrill voice of Donna Matilde piercing the window blinds, which were closed for mourning.

'They shot him!'

In the courtyard, Mimì the manservant informed him that nobody in the household had been able to get any sleep because of the marchesa's constant screaming. Without batting an eye, the marquis got back on his horse, according himself another seven days of special leave with Trisina, which would continue the process of turning Natale Pirrotta the field watcher into some sort of unlucky traveller. And it was his own fault, really, for wanting to keep up appearances, even in front of the crickets – like the time when, returning home earlier than planned, he had found his wife and his master together in bed, stark naked. As if it was the most natural thing in the world, Natale reported what he had to report, and then asked:

'Do you know where my wife Trisina might happen to be, sir?'

'I think she's in the garden,' the marquis replied, playing by the rules.

'I'll go and see if I can find her,' Pirrotta said, and went out.

'Well, since for that fool I'm in the garden, let me pick this nice big cucumber here,' Trisina said, laughing and grabbing him firmly under the sheets.

A sudden, violent cuff to the head from the marquis sent her flying out of the bed.

'You must never make fun of your husband. You must show him the respect he deserves.'

Before taking refuge again in Pirrotta's cottage and Trisina's lush garden, the marquis went into town, to the shop of Salamone e Vinci, fine jewellers. Without responding to the two business partners' hand-wringing condolences, he sat himself down in front of Salamone's counter. (He wanted nothing to do with Vinci – not because he wasn't as accomplished as his associate, but because for no apparent reason the man got on his nerves.) He then extracted five spent bullets from his pocket and laid them on the table.

'Have no fear,' he said, noticing the look on the jeweller's face, 'I fired them myself at a tree on my way here, and then dug them out with a knife.'

'And what do you want me to do?'

'Allow me to explain.'

Seeing him enter her room, confidently pull up an arm-chair, and sit down before her as she sat sunk in another armchair, Donna Matilde got flustered. Then she decided to talk to the stranger.

'Are you aware that my son was murdered?'

Don Filippo was not surprised. 'Ntontò had told him that the poor woman had not recognized anybody for the past month and used the formal mode of address with everyone. 'And how do you deal with it?' he had asked his daughter.

'I answer her in kind,' 'Ntontò had said, giving a wan hint of a smile, 'and follow the rules of etiquette to a T.'

'And you know what takes the cake?' the marchesa continued, speaking to the stranger. 'Nobody believes it. They say he was poisoned by a mushroom. My son, who knew everything there was to know about every mushroom in creation. Are you from these parts?'

'Who?' asked the marquis, taken by surprise.

'You. Are you from these parts?'

'No. Just passing through.'

And he really did feel as if he was only passing through, since the moment he had set foot back in his house he had come to the decision to grant himself another three months at Le Zubbie.

'I'm a friend of your husband, the marquis,' he added.

'The cuckolded bastard,' Donna Matilde said under her breath.

The marquis gave a start and grimaced.

'Do you mean that in a manner of speaking, or is it true?'

'Why are you making that face? His own brother wouldn't have such a reaction!'

'Marchesa, do not change the subject. You absolutely must answer my question.'

'I meant it in a manner of speaking. Happy now?' And she smiled a distant smile, as if, in the devastated landscape of her memory, a tiny, happy island had suddenly appeared.

Troubled, but afraid to take things any further, the marquis decided to come to the point.

'Your husband the marquis had a post-mortem performed on Rico.'

'What does that mean?'

'It means they had a look inside him. And they found these.'

He pulled out a large jewel case and opened it. A gold necklace sparkled inside, studded with gemstones and with lead.

'See these? They're the five bullets that were found in Rico's body. Your husband had them mounted. You were right all along, Marchesa. He was shot.'

'How beautiful,' said Donna Matilde, picking up the necklace, drawn to the glitter like a magpie and forgetting her victory – that is, the confirmation that her son died in the manner she had always maintained.

'My respects, Marchesa.'

Having made a proper bow, Don Filippo was about to withdraw when he was stopped by his wife's voice.

'Is that gentleman with you?'

'What gentleman?' said the marquis, looking around and seeing no one.

'Why, that one there,' the marchesa replied with irritation, pointing at the cat, Mustafà, who was asleep at the foot of the bed.

'No, that gentleman came in on his own.'

In the corridor, as he was heading towards his room, Don Filippo stopped short, seized by a sudden idea.

'If my wife can no longer distinguish between a cat and a man, why would she be able to distinguish between a goat and a woman? I think, one of these days, I will bring Carmelina home with me and introduce her to Matilde. I'll tell her she was Rico's secret fiancée, and she should treat her like a daughter.'

'That makes three games in a row you've lost, Marquis. You seem a bit distracted. What's on your mind?'

'A goat.'

'A goat goat?'

'That's right.'

Baron Uccello felt sorry for his friend. Apparently the marquis was having trouble getting over the loss of his son. They played another game, also won by the baron.

'I think it's not my day,' said Don Filippo, and he added, 'I wanted to ask you something, my friend. It's a private matter, and you must feel absolutely free not to answer.'

'Let's hear it.'

'Are you fond of your two daughters-in-law?'

'I don't know why you're asking me this, and I don't want to know. But I will answer. You see, when Sarina, my elder son's wife, comes to see me, I fall into a trance just looking at her and I cannot keep myself from sighing from time to time. If she ever happens to want anything, I am ready to oblige her. And when she thanks me in that sweet little voice of hers, I melt. With Luisina, my younger son's wife, it's something else entirely, by God!'

'Are you not fond of her?'

The baron looked around, took his chair, moved it, and sat down beside Don Filippo so he could speak softly. 'I'm going to tell you something in confidence that I'm embarrassed to admit, and so I don't want you looking at me when I say it. A few nights ago I had a dream about Luisina, and we had just finished doing what a man and a woman do together, if you know what I mean. The moonlight was filtering through the shutter as I lay there contemplating her naked, white body. This, old boy, is just to give you an idea.'

He paused.

'You, unfortunately, will never know this, but a father always falls in love with his son's beloved.'

At that moment the marquis saw her in the clearing at the edge of the wood: the fine white-and-brown Agrigento long-haired nanny goat, with big moist frightened eyes, coiling horns like a unicorn's, and a sweet, sweet udder the colour of baked bread. And through this vision of Carmelina, the marquis understood in a flash what his son was about, and what, as a man, he had lost in losing him. For the first time since the misfortune, a genuine feeling of utter grief rose up inside him and tore him apart.

That evening, as 'Ntontò and Don Filippo were eating the supper cooked by the maid Peppinella and her husband Mimì, an ex-highwayman and convict taken into their home by the marquis's father out of pure compassion, Don Filippo could not take his eyes off his daughter. The black of mourning became her; she looked like a sugar doll, plump as a quail with her generous hips, long blonde hair, rosy cheeks, and blue, somewhat crazed eyes.

'But who does she take after?' the marquis wondered, himself being swarthy as a crow, as was Donna Matilde.

He quickly dispelled the question, remembering his wife's enigmatic smile.

'Has Mama eaten?' 'Ntontò asked Peppinella.

'Not much, but she did eat,' replied the maid. Donna Matilde no longer wanted to leave her room for anything in the world.

Even her voice is beautiful, thought the marquis. Then he addressed her directly.

'So, tell me, why don't you want to get married? You've certainly had some good offers.'

'I don't want to settle down just yet.'

'And when will you, my dear? Don't forget, you're almost twenty-five, and in these parts—'

'So now you suddenly want to play the patriarch?' 'Ntontò snapped. 'After blithely shrugging it off your whole life?'

The marquis did not react, and they continued their meal in silence.

'That was a nice necklace you gave Mama,' 'Ntontò said a few minutes later, to lift the pall that had fallen over them. 'But why did you have them mount five pieces of lead in it?'

'I told her those were the bullets that killed Rico.'

'But Rico was killed by mushrooms!'

'I know, but I decided to prove her right in her obsession by telling her a lie.'

'But why?'

'Because now, you'll see, she'll calm down. She'll stop screaming, and we'll be able to sleep at night again.'

Instead, it was a night of horror. Flung sideways across the double bed, the marquis had been dead to the world for some two hours when something grazed his cheek. Thinking it was a *pelacchio*, one of those big flying cockroaches that fill the air like flocks of swallows during the hot Sicilian summers, he dealt himself a such a slap that it completely woke him up. Opening his eyes, Don Filippo saw, in the faint light of a small lamp he kept burning at night, a white shape standing at the foot of the bed. The marquis was a superficial but temperamental man, and thus as prone to acts of heedless bravery as to those of repulsive cowardice. Tonight it was his chicken-hearted side that went into action. In a twinkling, and for no reason whatsoever, he was convinced that the white figure before him was Rico's ghost. He became drenched in sweat.

'What do you want? What have I done to you?' he began imploring, kneeling in bed, hands folded. 'Take pity on me!' Seeing that the ghost wasn't answering him, and remembering that these shades from the afterlife abhorred light, the marquis managed, after several attempts thwarted by the tremor in his hands, to light the oil lamp on his bedside table. Instead of disappearing, however, the shape acquired substance in the person of a barefoot

Donna Matilde in her nightgown, hair loose, eyes glistening, all made up and looking twenty years younger than her age.

'I wanted to thank you,' said the marchesa, 'for the present you took the trouble to bring me.'

She fell silent, as Don Filippo looked on, flummoxed at finding her so youthful as to enflame his desire. Then Donna Matilde continued:

'But it wasn't only to thank you that I disturbed your sleep.'

'I am at your service,' said Don Filippo, and he made room for her beside him in the bed. In so doing, however, his mood darkened. How dare his wife enter the bedroom of someone who was a stranger to her, at night, and with unmistakable intentions to boot? But he was dead wrong as to her intentions.

'What I wanted to ask you, sir, was this. Do you know the name of the person who shot my son?'

'His name? I'm afraid not. It must have been someone who didn't like him.'

'No one could ever dislike Rico.'

The marquis reflected that if he gave her a name, any name at all, she would go quietly back to bed, and he could go back to sleep.

'All right. His name is Abdul. He's an Arab who lives out by Trapani.'

'And why did he kill Rico?'

'He belongs to a sect of fanatics who kill twenty-two-year-old men called Federico who eat mushrooms.'

'Thank you. You're very kind. Will you be staying with us?'

'Just a little while longer.'

'Then I'll say goodbye, because I'm leaving tomorrow.'

'And where are you going, Marchesa?'

'Out Trapani way. And the minute I see him, I'm going to shoot that Arab. With this.'

All the while she had been keeping her right arm behind her back. Now that arm reached out towards the marquis. In her right hand Donna Matilde was tightly gripping a large pistol and aiming it straight at him. At this point that other aspect of Don Filippo's character, his temerity, came to the fore. Emitting a yell that would have frightened a wolf, the marquis leapt at his wife and seized the wrist of the hand holding the gun. They rolled about on the floor. A first shot was fired, shattering the lamp, spilling the oil onto the bed and setting the sheets ablaze. The two continued grappling, squawking and yelping as they struggled. The second shot went towards the door through which Mimì was entering at that exact moment. Recovering his former highwayman's instincts, the manservant, judging from the report alone, was able to calculate the angle and distance, and stepped aside just enough to dodge the bullet. 'Ntontò and Peppinella also came running, and the two antagonists were finally separated.

'This man jumped on me, wanting to do lewd things to me, and pointed a gun at me,' said Donna Matilda, perfectly calm, and all in one breath.

'Me?! It was you who pointed the gun at me, you liar!'

'How dare you speak to me that way, you scoundrel!'

'Ntontò and Peppinella led the marchesa away and locked her in her room, then rushed back to help Don Filippo and Mimì put out the spreading fire. It kept them busy until morning.

'Everything all right at home?' asked Baron Uccello.

'Yes, why do you ask?' shot back the marquis, who was losing his third game of the morning.

'Well, it's just that people in town are gossiping.'

'What about?'

'That late at night they heard two shots inside your house and saw flames through the shutters.'

'Why don't people in this town sleep at night and peddle their own fish?'

'Dunno. They say there were two shots from a rifle . . . or maybe a pistol.'

'That was me, my friend. I'd bought two rockets to set off on San Calorio's day, but then I couldn't do it because we were in mourning. So I tried them at home.'

'In the middle of the night?'

'Why, is there a specific time of day or night for setting off rockets at home?'

It was no use. The marquis sat at his desk, with Gegè Papìa the accountant, the administrator of the estate, beside him, putting papers in front of him to sign. And before writing each signature, Don Filippo sniffed his fingers. It was no use. He had washed his hands repeatedly, but the smell of Donna Matilde's skin remained stuck to his hands, arms, all over. They had clung to each other too long during their struggle. Don Filippo signed the last document. The Pelusos were, in a sense, traitors to their class and wealth: they knew how to read and write, whereas the majority of Sicilian nobles customarily signed with an X. 'He won't sign because he's noble,' they would say. Reading and writing were for miserable paper-pushers and clerks. Papìa bowed and went out, leaving Don Filippo to sniff himself undisturbed.

After knocking lightly, 'Ntontò came in.

'Did you tell Papìa to pay for Grandfather's and Rico's funerals?' she asked. 'Father Macaluso reminded me again this morning. Papìa never wants to give a penny to priests, not even at knifepoint.'

'Yes, I told him. The church will be paid this very day. But while you're here, 'Ntontò, tell me something: does Mama still have the curse?'

'Ntontò immediately took offence.

'How can you make light of these things at a time like this? She's in distress, not cursed!'

'You misunderstood me. I meant, does Mama still have her periods?'

'Ntontò turned bright red.

'What kind of filth have you got in your head? Mama stopped being a woman two years ago!'

She burst into tears and ran out of the room. Don Filippo went back to smelling his hands.

It was a second straight night of hell. His wife's scent had grown even stronger on his naked body, bringing back memories of nights twenty years earlier, when he and Donna Matilde had grappled together for more pleasant reasons. And the burnt smell lingering on the walls made him cough, but he didn't feel like getting up and going into another bedroom. He blamed his agitation on the intense heat that still prevailed, though it was late September. When, at last, he heard the church bells calling for morning Mass, he got dressed and slipped out with a light step, closing the front door behind him without a sound.

Standing at the back of the church, he waited for Mass to end and for four old women and two peasants hunched from working the land to go out, whereupon he raced into the sacristy. Father Macaluso, who was removing his vestments with the help of the sacristan, must certainly have been surprised to see him, but pretended to pay no notice. Surly and hot-tempered as he was by nature, he was waiting for the marquis to greet him first, while Don Filippo, for his part, was not about to open the proceedings by addressing a priest who was the son of clay-footed peasants. So in the end neither greeted the other. And just to spite the nobleman, Father Macaluso folded and refolded his vestments five times more than was necessary.

'Stew in your own juices, fool.'

After showing the sacristan out, the priest finally looked at the marquis.

'What is it?'

'I'd like to speak to you.'

'Ah, thank goodness. I thought you were here to give me a shave.'

The marquis didn't react.

'And I would also like what I'm about to tell you to remain a secret.'

'Look, I don't usually discuss things people tell me. But if you want to feel more certain, entrust yourself to the secrecy of the confessional. What do you have to say to me?'

'I would like to speak to man to man.'

'Let's have it.'

'I want a son.'

'Good God, that again?'

'What do you mean, "That again"?'

'Look, I was made priest of this parish, replacing the late Father Carnazza, bless his soul, at the very moment when you got it into your head that you had to have a son. And the marchesa would come to confess to me every Saturday. Have I made myself clear?'

'Like hell.'

'No, what's like hell is the torment you put that poor woman through every night the Lord sent your way!'

'But isn't that what marriage is for?'

'Yes, indeed, for that, among other things. But not for satisfying your egotism and vanity. You wanted a son who could inherit your name and estate. But what is a name, in your opinion? What are earthly possessions? They are shit, that's what they are.'

'Excuse me, but if I enjoy dancing in shit, what's it to you?'

'Let's drop it. What do you want from me?'

'Listen, before continuing, I'll tell you something I'm under no obligation to tell you. You're wrong about my wanting an heir. For Rico, yes, that was true. But this next son I want the same way any man without a penny in his pocket would.'

'That is to your credit. But I don't think Donna Matilde is capable any longer.'

'Whoever mentioned my wife?'

The priest blinked. 'Did I hear correctly?'

'Perfectly.'

Father Macaluso turned into a pepper, half red, half green.

'Jesus bloody Christ, you come here, into the house of the Lord, to tell me you want to commit adultery?'

'Come now, adultery! Let's not exaggerate. I will have a son with another woman, since with my own wife, by your own admission, I cannot. Then I'll adopt the kid and that's the last you'll ever hear of it.'

'It would still be adultery, so long as Donna Matilde is alive! When the poor lady ascends at last into heaven, only then, after a proper period of mourning, could you marry the woman with whom you wish to sire a son, and then all would be in order.'

'The fact is that the woman I want to bear my son is already married.'

'Then, by hook or by crook, you are hell-bent on committing adultery! You are obsessed, an adulterous maniac! Don't you know it is a more grievous sin than murder?'

'Are you joking?'

'I am not, you idiot!' yelled Father Macaluso, choking on his rage. And, picking up a very heavy chair, he did not spare the marquis a parting shot:

'Leave this house of God at once, you piece of shit!'

Three

It took the marquis only a few days to arrange things. He granted power of attorney to Papìa the accountant, had four trunks loaded onto two mules, and headed off to Le Zubbie. When Natale Pirrotta saw him arrive and take heavy clothing out of the trunks, woollen sweaters and overcoats, he darkened. 'You'll have to excuse me, your excellency, but if your intention is to spend the winter here, what am I supposed to do? Go round and round Sicily like a spinning top?'

'No need to worry, Natà. Tomorrow Peppinella's elder sister Maddalena will be arriving, who's seventy years old. She'll sleep with Trisina, to keep the tongues from wagging.'

'And where am I supposed to go?'

'You're going to go and lend a hand to Sasà Ragona, the field watcher of Pian dei Cavalli. He's ill with malaria and can't work like before. And you can come back here to see Trisina whenever you want.'

The marquis didn't return to his own home until Christmas Eve. The first thing he noticed was that there was no crib in the family chapel.

'Have you forgotten?' said 'Ntontò. 'It was Rico who used to make the crib. I don't know how to, and neither does Mimì.'

Don Filippo thought back to Rico's Nativity scenes. Yes, they had little mountains made of porous lava, palm trees, a rivulet, a cave, the ox and the donkey, but everything was drowned in a thick carpet of mushrooms. And the Baby Jesus was himself a mushroom, between the mushrooms of Joseph and Mary.

'Is Mama awake?'

At 'Ntontò's affirmative nod, he opened the door, but was forced to take a step back by the smell.

'Jesus, can't you open a window?'

'She doesn't want me to.'

Overcoming his nausea, he went in and sat down in front of his wife.

She had become an old woman in the space of three months, her hair now completely white. It was difficult to see in her room. With the flame of the oil lamp kept low, Donna Matilde squinted as she tried to make out the features of her visitor's face. To help her out, Don Filippo went over to the chest of drawers, turned up the flame, and sat back down. Then the marchesa recognized him.

'Help!' she began to shout. 'Help! For heaven's sake, somebody please help!'

'Ntontò, Peppinella, and Mimì came running and the usual pandemonium broke out. With the strength of her desperation, Donna Matilde managed to stand up halfway from the chair, gripping the arms.

'It's him! The man who wanted to shoot me! Who wanted to do lewd things to me!'

Before leaving the room, Don Filippo turned around to look at his wife. And it seemed to him — but surely it wasn't possible, it must have been an effect of the dancing light of the oil lamp — like she was laughing.

'We're going to put Mama to bed, and then we're going out,' said 'Ntontò. 'We're going to midnight Mass: me, Peppinella, and Mimì.'

'Mimì, too?'

'Yes.'

'I'm sure he'll have to attend quite a few Masses before he atones for all his sins.'

'What are you going to do, Papà? Go to the club?'

'I don't know yet.'

He sat for a long time at the now cleared table, sipping his wine every so often. Then, when he was certain that everyone was gone, he headed for Rico's room. It was years since he had last set foot in it, and it was much smaller than he remembered. He put the lamp down on a table and looked around. It all gave him a strange feeling he couldn't explain, and the more he looked at things, the stronger the impression became. Suddenly he understood. This was the bedroom of a grown man; one could see it in the size of the bed, the clothes, the shoes, and the shotgun propped in a corner, which Bonocore had apparently recovered from the woods. Yet at the same time it was also the bedroom of a little boy, an impression that came from the drawings stuck to the wall, which Rico had recently made and which portrayed, in infantile fashion, 'Papà', 'Mama', and 'My sister 'Ntontò', going by the words written under each picture. Don Filippo opened the desk drawer and found a stack of paper, every sheet covered with drawings of the same subject: a goat. Looking at them one by one, the marquis could see just how diligently Rico had begun to make progress; in fact, the last sheet was a genuine portrait of Carmelina.

Rico had coloured it and even got the shadings right. In a sudden fit of anger of which he was hardly aware, he tossed the sheet into the air and went out.

'What kind of bloody Christmas Eve is this?' he asked himself. 'I think I'll go to the club and gamble one of my properties.'

He felt overcome with fatigue, however, and his shoulders ached as if he had been carrying a heavy load. Very slowly he opened the door to Donna Matilde's room and looked inside. Only one small lamp was lit, and he felt reassured. He didn't want there to be much light. If his wife saw him and recognized him, she was liable to start another riot.

He sat down in an armchair at the foot of the bed.

Donna Matilde was sleeping with her mouth open, and every now and then she emitted a moan. Don Filippo slowly reached out and rested his hand on his wife's cheek; then he withdrew it, brought it to his nose, and inhaled. Nothing. His hand smelled only of rancid sweat. He stayed a little while longer, watching Donna Matilde, then spoke to her.

'I'm going to spend the night with you. Merry Christmas, Matì.'

When 'Ntontò, back from Mass, went to check on her mother, she saw Don Filippo asleep. She didn't wake him.

The marquis took the road to Le Zubbie at a gallop, as if he was being pursued, and arrived in such a rush in front of the house that he very nearly frightened to death Trisina, Maddalena, and Pirrotta, who was saying goodbye to the two women before heading back to Pian dei Cavalli.

'Natà, can't you leave tomorrow morning? You need to explain something to me.'

That evening, after supper, the two men sat down near

the well, and the marquis asked Pirrotta how he could build himself a small fireplace in his bedroom.

'Why don't you hire a mason?'

'Because I want to make it with my own hands. Don't worry, I can do it. Anyway, it'll help me pass the time.'

'But you have to climb up on the roof, which is dangerous. My poor wife certainly learned that.'

'Pirrò, I want to do it my way. Have you got the necessary tools?'

'You'll find everything you need in the house.'

After listening to Pirrotta's instructions, the marquis felt sleepy. He said goodbye to his field watcher, who would be leaving at daybreak and would sleep in the stable so as not to disturb the two women. Then he withdrew to his room. He sat for a short while at the window, smoking his pipe, and when his eyelids began to droop, he went to bed. But, as if cursed, once horizontal he no longer felt sleepy. For hours he tossed and turned, with the sheets twisting around his sweaty body. He finally became convinced that the only thing to do was to return to the window and watch the morning star. He heard Pirrotta in the stable, saddling the mule and then leaving. He waited until the dawn light allowed him to see the line of the sea in the distance, and then he lay back down, eyes wide open, hands crossed behind his head. Such was his position when Trisina came in, lay down beside him, and began kissing him through the hairs in his armpit.

'We have all the time we want,' she said. 'I drugged the old woman.'

'You did what?'

'I put a little poppy extract in her soup.'

'Won't that hurt her?'

'No, your excellency. I tried it once when you weren't here. It only makes her sleep late in the morning. And she'll complain she has a little headache.'

She began groping him and started laughing.

'Your excellency! Are you drugged, too? Let me wake it up for you, the way my lord likes best.'

She pulled away the sheet and started sliding down the marquis's body, but he grabbed her by the hair to stop her.

'Let it be,' he said. 'It's feeling a little melancholy this morning.'

Donna Matilde made her decision around the middle of January. She had just been brought lunch, which was put down on a little table in front of her armchair, when 'Ntontò heard a tremendous crash in her mother's room. Going in, she found the little table overturned and the broth and soft-boiled egg dripping from the broken plates and onto the rug.

'Did it fall?'

'Nnh-unh.'

'What happened, then?'

'I did it. On purpose.'

'Why?'

'I got fed up.'

'With the food?'

'Nnh-unh.'

'With sitting down?'

'Nnh-unh.'

'With what, then?'

'With everything.'

And from that day forward there was no way to get her to swallow anything. She took to her bed, sustaining herself only with a little water in a glass on the bedside table, and she no longer wanted to talk to anyone, not even 'Ntontò. Dr Smecca, when he came to see her, threw up his hands.

'I'd been expecting this sooner or later. It's not that she's ill; she simply no longer wants to go on living.'

'Ntontò, however, wanted to give it one more try and sent for Fofò La Matina. Polite and solicitous as ever, the pharmacist examined the marchesa, corroborated what Smecca had said, and returned to the pharmacy. He reappeared an hour later.

'We're going to do an experiment,' said Fofò, pouring the contents of a small envelope into Donna Matilde's glass. 'This should stimulate her appetite.'

But Donna Matilde's appetite did not return, and try as the pharmacist might with a variety of different-coloured powders, the result was always the same. In fact, when

Donna Matilde finally noticed changes in the taste of the water, she decided not to drink any more, but only to wet her lips with a handkerchief. At which point, Fofò La Matina, too, had to throw up his hands in front of 'Ntontò, who had no tears left to cry.

Don Filippo sat in front of his fireplace, glorying in his creation as if he had built the royal palace of Caserta, and warming himself up with Trisina on his lap. It was early evening. Maddalena had already gone to bed, duly drugged, so there was no danger of surprises. The surprise came instead when the marquis heard someone calling him from the yard. Armed with a rifle, he cautiously opened the window and shutters.

'It's me, your excellency. Mimì.'

'What is it?'

'You must come into town. I brought the caleche. The marchesa is dying.'

They left, with Mimì blindly lashing the horse all the way.

'I'm afraid we'll be too late.'

When he entered his wife's bedroom, the marquis was immediately shot in the middle of the forehead by a dirty look from Father Macaluso, who was reciting prayers accompanied by 'Ntontò and Peppinella, who were kneeling at the foot of the bed.

'Is she alive?' he asked.

Fofò La Matina, who was standing by the window, nodded yes.

'I want you all out of here,' said the marquis. 'I'll let you know when you can come back in.'

They obeyed. Raindrops began to patter against the windows as Don Filippo took a chair to sit down in at the head of the bed. Then, bending slightly forward, he took his wife's hand in his. He stayed that way for a while. Then he had the impression that there was a leak in the roof and that rain was filtering inside. Looking up, he saw that the ceiling was intact.

'Ah, well,' he said to himself, 'that must mean I'm crying.'

Instead of letting Fofò La Matina into his wife's bedroom, Don Filippo stopped him in the doorway. 'Do you really need to be here?'

He led him into his office, sat him down on a sofa, offered him a cigar, which was declined, and lit his pipe.

'Do you mind if I speak informally with you? I've known you since you were about ten years old.'

'I'm honoured, your excellency.'

'And don't call me "your excellency" or "marquis". Just call me "Don Filippo".'

'As you wish.'

'Forgive me, but I feel I need to talk to somebody.'

'Here I am.'

'You know something? It was I, in a sense, who made your father's fortune.'

'Please excuse me,' said a young Filippo Peluso, barely more than twenty, as he began to rise, huffing and twisting and muttering as much as was necessary to lift his twenty stone of flesh and bones into a vertical position. 'I'm going to take advantage of this little pause while my friend Uccello is dealing.'

They were playing briscola, the young versus the old. The young were Peluso and Uccello, the old, Marquis Fiannaca and Don Gregorio Gulisano.

'And that makes four, dammit,' Gulisano commented under his breath. As someone who weighed barely seven stone, he felt a sort of dull, irrational irritation whenever Filippo Peluso began his manoeuvres to stand up.

'Why, do I have to pay a toll?' said the marchesino, who was keen of hearing.

'For what?'

'For pissing. For the last hour you've been counting how many times I get up.'

'I only wonder why someone would have to go to the toilet four times in two hours,' Gulisano snapped back, turning green in the face.

'Come on, gentlemen, let's be serious,' Baronello Uccello cut in. 'If you start arguing, we'll never finish this blessed game. And I have to be home at the stroke of midnight.'

'You can go right now, if you like; the door is open.'

'Come now, Marquis . . .'

'Come now, Marquis, bollocks. We're going to be here till morning if Mr Gulisano doesn't explain to me exactly why it bothers him so much when I feel the need to urinate. What, does the toilet belong to him? Is he afraid I'm going to fill it up?'

Gregorio Gulisano, visibly making an effort to remain calm, opened his mouth, took a breath, but said not a word. Silence descended. Marchesino Peluso didn't budge, one hand gripping the back of his chair, the other leaning heavily on the card table; Marquis Fiannaca was counting and recounting the gold and silver pieces he had in front of him, while young Uccello kept cutting the deck. After a suitable pause, Filippo Peluso continued:

'Either Mr Gulisano deigns to explain himself, or in one minute, since I can no longer hold it in, I'm going to whip it out and inundate the whole table.'

In the face of this threat — which, given the young Peluso's capriciousness and bright ideas, was not at all a hollow one — Marquis Fiannaca decided to intervene.

'My dear Gulisano,' he said, 'would you please do me a personal favour and clarify your attitude for our friend Peluso? That way, we can forget about it and go back to our game.'

Fiannaca was a good, kind man of few words and sound judgement, but it was known far and wide that it was unwise to deny his requests.

'Because it makes me angry,' Gregorio Gulisano explained between clenched teeth. 'How can this be? For years he's been boring us with the fact that his difficulty in urination makes him fat as a pig, he tells us in such great detail about the medical examination he got in Palermo

*that it's coming out of our ears for two days, he explains how he can
only fuck when he's lying on his back and not like the rest of the human
race, and then he comes here tonight and starts pissing every half an
hour, so that I can't follow the game any more.'*

*'And you, Marquis, how do you explain it?' asked Fiannaca, con-
tinuing his mediation.*

*'It's all because of four miraculous pears that Santo La Matina gave
my father. And now, with your leave, may I?'*

'And there you have it,' Don Filippo concluded. 'That was
how your father, who worked a parcel of our land as a
tenant, became known. My father and yours liked each
other very much and often talked. And when Santo found
out that I was so fat that I had trouble moving, he said he
had a remedy for it, and sent me the pears. Then, when I
ran out of pears, I went personally to ask for more. And
so the two of us set out from your house and rode for two
hours, going out past Crasto Mountain and finally up
Dead Man's Mountain. It was a desolate spot; even snakes
avoided it. We started descending the slope, which was all
rocks, and at one point the valley was blocked by a great
many boulders. We tied up the horses and slid into a
hole. Coming out on the other side, I thought I was in
the Garden of Eden. It was barely two acres of land, but
it had everything: nectarines, tiny pears, sorbs, peaches,
oranges, lemons, grapes, sweet almonds, bitter almonds,
pistachios, as well as chickpeas still green, tomatoes, beans,

peas . . . There they were, all these things, one beside the other, in profusion, regardless of the season. How the hell Santo did this, only he knew.'

'He used to fuck the ground and make love to the plants,' Fofò said calmly, after listening impassively to Don Filippo's reminiscence.

'Are you kidding me?'

'I would never kid you, Don Filippo. I'm telling you something I've never told anyone else. I once saw it with my own eyes, when I was pretending to be asleep. He would make an opening in the ground or the trunk of a tree and fuck it. He used his sperm as fertilizer. But he didn't do it all the time, only on certain nights when a crow he used to talk to would tell him to do it.'

'He used to talk to a bird?!'

'Well, as far as that goes, he also spoke to ants, snakes, lizards, you name it. At first my father seemed batty to me; I thought he was talking to himself.'

'Why is someone who talks to crickets not batty, in your opinion?' asked Don Filippo, polemically holding fast to natural reason.

'But, you see, Don Filippo, the fact is, the animals would answer him.'

'They talked?'

'No, they didn't actually talk. But they would reply in their own way, with a movement of the body or a sound of their own. But he alone could understand what they were saying. Once, under a scorching sun, he had a three-hour discussion with a lizard.'

Upon hearing this, Don Filippo felt his head begin to spin. He decided to steer the conversation onto more solid ground.

'So, I was saying how your father's name came to be known. And I should mention that that snake Gulisano had secretly followed me. When I came back to town with my pears, Gulisano, with typical cheek, introduced himself to Santo and said and did what he needed to do so that Santo gave him four fennel bulbs to make him gain weight. In three months' time, Gulisano and I had both become fashion plates. But the rumour began to spread, and soon everybody started asking Santo for things. Your father didn't know how to say no, but since he was afraid the garden's location might be discovered, he would send you into town three times a week to deliver the necessary things to the people who needed them. Do you remember what they used to call you?'

'Yes. The balcony squirt.'

'You were always walking around looking up at the little girls on the balconies and crashing into things. One time I found you planted under one of the windows of this house, and there was 'Ntontò, not yet eight years old, and you were looking at her, spellbound. But she was looking at you, too. I gave you such a kick in the arse, you must have flown ten feet. The tomatoes you were carrying in your basket spilled all over the ground, and you started crying. Do you remember?'

'No. I got kicked so many times in those days, my arse still hurts.'

Don Filippo heaved a long sigh.

'I'm getting old, my friend,' he said. 'I'm starting to talk about times gone by.'

And they waited in silence for Donna Matilde to die.

Two hours after the funeral, Don Filippo, having taken to his heels, was already on his horse, preparing to return to Le Zubbie. Mimì, holding the animal by the reins, led his master out of the stable to the exit, then locked the door behind him.

Before applying the spurs, the marquis stopped to look back. On the right half of the double door hung three conspicuous signs of mourning: three black rosettes – the first one discoloured by the sun, the second a bit less, the third brand-new. Under the first was a scroll with the words 'For my dear father'; under the second, the words 'For my beloved son'; and under the third, only three words: 'For my wife'.

'At least there was still some space left,' the marquis thought as he rode off.

In the sixteen months of life that remained to him, Don Filippo spent his days peacefully. There was nothing for him to do at Le Zubbie except to sleep with Trisina and take long walks. Thus it happened one day, as he was walking through his vineyard, one row at a time, he made a distressing discovery. He waited for Pirrotta to return from one of his ever more far-flung journeys to speak to him about it.

'Natà, have you seen the vines?'

'No, since I'm not the one looking after them.'

'Come with me.'

Pirrotta's expert eye immediately recognized the damage.

'They've caught the disease,' he said. 'They need a sulphur treatment.'

'Well, why don't you give them one?'

'Because it would take many days of work. And I don't want to sleep under the same roof as Trisina.'

Don Filippo eyed him thoughtfully.

'I think we can find a solution to that.'

Natale Pirrotta accepted the solution suggested by the marquis, but only because the diseased vines made his heart ache. The arrangement thought up by Don Filippo was very simple. If Natale didn't want to sleep under the same roof as Trisina, they needed only build a room, with its own roof, beside the main house, for him. It seemed a reasonable proposition to the field watcher, who with great gusto got down to work on the stones, sand, and lime. The door and window arrived on a horse-drawn cart driven by Mimì. Some twenty days later, Pirrotta was able to sleep in his new annexe. And Maddalena, Peppinella's sister, was sent back to Palazzo Peluso in Vigàta to accompany Miss 'Ntontò on those rare occasions when she left home to go to church. At Le Zubbie, the rules were always respected: after the evening meal, Pirrotta would go and sleep in his room on the ground floor, Trisina would go upstairs to the master bedroom with twin beds, and the marquis would withdraw to his own. What went on between Don Filippo and Trisina after the lamps were extinguished, only God, Pirrotta, and all of Vigàta knew.

One evening after Trisina had gone to bed, as they were smoking their pipes and watching the moon, the marquis decided to reveal his intentions to Natale.

'Natà,' he said, 'I want to have a son.'

'With Trisina?'

'No, with you.'

They laughed.

'So where do I come in?' Pirrotta asked, after a pause.

'You're going to play the father. You'll take this son into your home and give him your name. Then I, who in the eyes of the world have no male heir, will adopt the boy, with your consent. Does that sound reasonable to you?'

'As for sounding reasonable, it sounds reasonable. But have you talked to Trisina about it?'

'Who the hell cares what Trisina thinks? She'll do what the two of us tell her to do, if we're in agreement.'

Pirrotta remained silent a long time, pondering the matter. The marquis misinterpreted his field watcher's silence.

'We both stand to gain from this, Natà. I'll have my son, and you can pocket as much as you want for allowing me to adopt him. As much as you want.'

Pirrotta removed the pipe slowly from his mouth.

'I have always respected you. And you have always respected me. Why do you want to start offending me now?'

'Please forgive me, Natà,' said the marquis, realizing the mistake he had made.

'Let me think it over tonight, and tomorrow I'll tell you what I've decided.'

The following morning, an exchange of glances, without any words, was all that needed. The marquis understood that he had Pirrotta's permission.

Four

The only clamour and commotion that Le Zubbie ever saw came with the September grape harvest. Throngs of noisy women would arrive at daybreak, having been picked up at the gates of Vigàta by two dozen carts, and get straight down to work. Each woman would take a row of vines and, squatting with knife in hand, would cut the bunches and then drop them into a sorghum basket. When the basket was full, she would empty it into a reed hamper, which she then hoisted onto her shoulders and upended into a cart with high side panels. Once full, the cart would head down the road to the hamlet of Durrueli, where the marquis had his presses, vats, barrels, and cellars; after delivering its load, it quickly retraced its path. In the spacious kitchen, Trisina and Maddalena — who had been summoned back for the occasion — prepared the *calatina*, that is, the food for the vine workers to eat with their bread: one day it was *macco*, a thick bean purée, another day it was *caponatina*, which was made of capers, celery, onions, and olives stewed in a little tomato sauce flavoured with a dash of vinegar. At twelve noon on the dot, Natale would blow the whistle, and the women would drop everything and scramble towards the great cauldron in the middle of the clearing. Maddelena would hand a hot bowl to each woman as she filed past. They ate, sang, talked, and gossiped, scolded each other for rudeness, and then half an hour later, they all raced back to the vineyard to work until just before sunset. Pirrotta would then give another whistle, and the women would hop onto the carts, dripping with grape juice, and return to Vigàta.

The marquis had a marvellous time, walking back and forth between the rows of vines, listening to the shouts the women exchanged with one another. He loved hearing the chatter, the profanities, the insinuations whose meaning was clearer than if stated outright. At one point he took a glancing knife-slash on his hand when he intervened in a scuffle between two women with weapons drawn. Trisina sucked the blood from the wound, then wrapped his hand in a piece of her nightgown, dispelling the marquis's anger over the incident and putting him in a jovial mood for the rest of the day.

On the last day of the harvest there was a tradition that had to be respected. One hundred baskets full of grapes were brought to a small press house behind the cottage, which had a shed beside it with a fermentation vat and a few casks. This was the field watcher's personal reserve of wine. Once this last task was finished, the women were paid by Natale and taken back to town after saying goodbye to Don Filippo. If God granted good health and life to all, they would see one another again at next year's harvest. Maddalena also left with them. Now that the marquis had arranged everything with Pirrotta, he didn't want her in his hair.

The following morning Don Filippo got up late and didn't hear Trisina about the house. He went outside and circled around the back to the press house. There he found Trisina, whose job was to empty the baskets when full; Natale was working inside. The building consisted of a single room with a small window and a sloping floor, which was made of concrete. Along the lower edge of the floor was a drain that led to a hole into which the grape juice flowed. The hole in turn led into the fermentation vat. In one corner of the press house there was a levered winepress to squeeze out the last juices. When the marquis arrived, the floor was invisible, being completely covered with grapes. Naked but for a piece of cloth tied around his hips to hide his private parts, and wearing hobnailed boots on his feet, Pirrotta was treading the grapes, going around the room along the walls and stamping hard. His eyes were half closed.

'You have to excuse me, sir. I've been working since the crack of dawn and I'm very tired and a little drunk.

The smell of the grapes is so strong, it's like drinking five bottles of wine.'

Trisina didn't sit still for a minute, either. She kept cleaning the fine screen that covered the hole and prevented other things – peels, seeds, the hard parts of the clusters – from entering the fermentation vat, shovelling and stirring the grapes on the floor, the better for Natale to crush them, and piling the squashed grapes in a corner so that they could be squeezed in the press. Every so often she emptied new baskets onto the floor.

The marquis went out for a walk. By midday he was back for lunch, which Trisina had already prepared.

'Is Natale still in the press house?'

'No, sir. He doesn't feel so good. He's got a headache.'

'All right, then. After I've had a little nap, we'll lend him a hand.'

Around three in the afternoon, the marquis went to the press house, stripped down to his underpants, put on Natale's hobnailed boots, and began treading the grapes, with Trisina's help.

'Trisina, my head is spinning,' he said after working for two hours.

'It's the smell of the grapes,' said Trisina. 'Let me come and give you a hand.'

Before the marquis's beclouded eyes, she stripped naked, throwing her clothes out of the door, and came up behind him, laughing, pushing him in the back to spur him on.

Suddenly the marquis couldn't take it any more and slipped and fell flat on his bottom. Trisina started laughing, first softly, then louder and louder, her head thrown back, when suddenly a long jet squirted out between her spread thighs, foaming atop the juice of the grapes.

'What on earth are you doing?'

'I'm pissing, your excellency. Everybody does when they tread the grapes. They think it makes the wine come out better.'

Laughing all the while, she was having trouble articulating her words and started to slip. To avoid falling flat on her face, she leaned against a wall. Suddenly she stopped laughing and looked over at the marquis, her eyelids drooping, her mouth half open.

'Come here, your excellency.'

The marquis leapt at her, his body bent slightly at the knees, and began fucking her. When she felt him enter her, Trisina let out a wail and hopped up in the air, wrapping her legs around the marquis's hips. Feeling his back about to give out, Don Filippo remembered a proverb his father had told him: *Fùttiri addritta e camminari na rina, portanu l'omu a la rovina.* He had walked on sand and knew how tiring it was, and now, fucking while standing, he was experiencing the whole truth of the saying. But it didn't last long, because Trisina climbed off him, leaving the marquis in the lurch.

'Let's do it this way, your excellency.' She turned, bent over, and leaned her head against the wall, supporting herself with her hands. Don Filippo immediately got going again and gripped her hips tightly, given the slippery floor. Trisina started screaming in a way she had never done before, sounding like a dog being beaten. But her wailing and the thumping of her head against the wall, without a care as to whether she might hurt herself, got the marquis even more excited.

Sweaty and dead tired, Don Filippo collapsed on top of Trisina, who, unable to bear the weight, fell face down on the floor, with the marquis still on top. There they stayed, struggling to breathe, half drowned in grape juice.

'Where is Natale?' asked the marquis as they were eating.

'Only he knows,' replied Trisina. 'Probably out and about again. You know what he's like.'

But the marquis wasn't convinced. He got up from the table and went outside to Natale's bedroom. Finding the door open, he went inside. Natale was lying in bed, talking, eyes bulging. He said he had seen the sun fall into the well and a snake fifteen feet long come back out. He said other strange things, too: that Trisina wasn't a woman but only a cunt with two arms and two legs. Don Filippo put his hand on Natale's forehead and nearly burned himself.

He ran and called Trisina. 'The sun's got into his head,' she said. 'We have to call Donna Gnazia. I'll go and get her myself.'

'You're not going anywhere at this hour of the night. Tell me where she lives.'

The marquis was unfamiliar with his own estate and took twice as long to find Donna Gnazia as Trisina would have done.

Day was already dawning when he returned, on horseback, with a crone a hundred years old following behind him on a donkey. Taking her time, the old woman slowly tied her donkey, asked for a mug of hot milk, drank it, then went to see Pirrotta. It took her one glance to confirm Trisina's diagnosis. From a bag she had brought with her she extracted a handful of herbs, which she boiled in water. When the tincture was ready, she strained it, filled a basin with it, and had Pirrotta, now sitting in a chair, soak his feet in it. The crone then took a bowl and filled it with water. Into this she poured four or five drops of oil, which formed a single yellow spot; then she put the bowl on Natale's head, holding it there with one hand, closed her eyes, and started muttering some gibberish. Then, before the marquis's spellbound eyes, the spot of oil burst apart, breaking up into many little spots that arranged themselves in a circle along the rim of the bowl.

'It's done,' said the old woman. 'It worked.'

Thus was the sun removed from Pirrotta's head.

An hour later, the field watcher behaved as if nothing had happened.

'I'm very grateful to you for all your help,' said Pirrotta.

'I didn't do it for you, Pirrò, but for myself. If you die before my son is born, what the hell am I going to tell people? That you got Trisina pregnant in a séance?'

One night in late October, Trisina got into the marquis's bed, giggling more than usual.

'What's wrong with you? You're laughing like an addle-brain.'

'I can't help it, your excellency.'

'Well, try not to. When you laugh like that, I can't do it, you know. It goes soft.'

Trisina started thinking about things that had made her cry in the past, like the time she was eight years old and her mother accidentally locked her in a cupboard, or another time when she tore a brand-new dress on a milk-thorn bush.

When he noticed she had turned serious, Don Filippo mounted her.

'No, not like that,' said Trisina. 'I'm afraid you'll hurt me.'

'Why should it hurt you? We've done it this way a thousand times.'

'But now it's different, sir. You know what? You got me pregnant, that day in the press house.'

Don Filippo said nothing. He got out of bed, staggering to the left and right, made it as far as the window,
opened the shutters and fainted, falling to the floor like a
sack of potatoes.

The following morning he raced into Vigàta, singing at
the top of his lungs all the way. As a result, when he tried
to talk to people in town, he had no voice left. He explained that he had caught a chill at Le Zubbie. His first
visit was to the midwife, Mrs Schilirò, and he arranged for
her to come to Le Zubbie the following Sunday to examine Trisina. He would send Mimì for her with a carriage.

His second visit was to the pharmacy. 'I'm expecting a
son,' he said to Fofò.

'Congratulations,' said the pharmacist, looking him up
and down. 'It doesn't show.'

'This is no time for jokes, Fofò. This Sunday I want
you to come in the carriage with the midwife and examine
Natale Pirrotta's wife.'

'I'm sorry, Marquis, but why don't you ask Dr Smecca?
He has more experience with that sort of thing and knows
more than I do.'

'I don't trust Dr Smecca.'

It wasn't true. He certainly did trust Dr Smecca, but
he could not forget what Pirrotta had told him: that the
doctor had dipped his bread in Trisina's soup. And had in
fact been the first to do so.

'All right,' said the pharmacist. 'Have you already been to your house, Marquis?'

'I haven't had the time.'

'Your daughter has been ill. I've been looking after her myself.'

At the thought of seeing 'Ntontò still dressed all in black, Don Filippo decided he wasn't yet ready to meet her.

'Greetings to all,' he said, entering the Nobles' Club.

'What's new?'

After the riot of greetings, exclamations of delight, and embraces, Baron Uccello informed his friend of the only new development, aside from the detailed inventory of lamented passings.

'The pharmacist has been broken in,' said the baron.

'What do you mean, "broken in"?'

'Do you remember the time we talked about him here at the club? Well, since then, and up until last week, Fofò La Matina's situation had not changed: nary a woman.'

'But are you sure?'

'Cross my heart. Neither in Vigàta nor the provincial capital.'

'But how could he do without it?'

'Why, don't priests do the same?' interjected Fede the surveyor, a churchgoing man.

'Good God, please don't talk about priests to me,' said the baron. He continued: 'Anyway, last Saturday, Signora

Clelia, having learned from her maid that the pharmacist would not open his shop that day because he had to prepare some medicinal herbs, made herself up and went and knocked at his door. Fofò opened up and found the lady before him. He tried not to let her inside, but there was nothing doing. Signora Clelia insisted she urgently needed to be examined. To cut a long story short, she wasted no time; she reached out and grabbed him. The pharmacist froze. Didn't budge. Encouraged, the lady undid his trousers and pants and brought the thing out into the open. And that was when the pharmacist popped.'

'What do you mean, he "popped"?' asked Lieutenant Baldovino.

'You know, my friend,' the marquis explained, 'the way the bung pops when you fill the barrel too full of wine.'

'Later, in the two hours that followed, the pharmacist attended to the lady till his barrel was empty,' the baron continued. 'When Signora Clelia came out of the pharmacy, people say she looked like a cat with a full belly, purring down the street.'

Fate had decided that the marquis should hear talk of the pharmacist for the rest of the day. 'Ntontò continued where his friends from the club had left off, telling him how Fofò La Matina had devotedly and valiantly cured her of an influenza that threatened to turn into pneumonia, without asking a penny in return.

'But I acquitted myself of my debt just the same.'

The marquis eyed his daughter.

'Did you make him pop, too?'

'I don't know what you mean,' said Ntontò, her face a question mark. 'I had Mimì bring him two demijohns of good wine.'

The marquis kept eyeing her, finding her even more beautiful than when he had left her, a bit thinner and paler from illness.

'When are you going to take off the weeds?'

'They're supposed to last three years.'

'And what if I die in the meantime?'

'What are you saying?!'

'How are you going to show your grief then, if I die? You've given it all to the others, even your grief for me! You're all decked out in black, outside and inside!' He was yelling, and didn't know why he felt so angry. 'Ntontò burst into tears, the marquis following after her for a few steps.

'You can paint your bottom black, if I die!' he shouted. 'It can be your special way of mourning me!'

He had just woken up from his nap when Mimì arrived.

'The sacristan's here, your excellency. He's got a message for you from Father Macaluso.'

The marquis reluctantly got dressed and went into the anteroom.

'With your excellency's blessing,' said the sacristan.

'How many blessings do you want to extract? You're already taken care of by the priest. What do you want?'

'Father Macaluso says you should drop in to the church, at your excellency's convenience, of course.'

'And why should I drop in to the church? Tell Father Macaluso he should drop in to see me.'

After the sacristan had raced back and forth three or four times, the two parties reached an agreement. They would meet at six o'clock sharp in the square, between the church and the club. Naturally, they did not greet each other.

'I want to talk about your daughter,' said Father Macaluso, getting straight to the point.

'And why should I talk about her with you?'

'Because I'm a priest and I'm supposed to look after the souls of my parishioners.'

'You're asking me to discuss 'Ntontò's soul?'

'For the love of God, Marquis, don't make me lose my temper. You know how easily I get upset, and I might piss outside the urinal.'

'Well, you should know that if you piss outside the urinal, I'm liable to shit outside it.'

'I know. That's why I'm suggesting that we set off, both of us, on the right foot. All right?'

'All right.'

'Would you please explain to me what sort of life your

daughter leads? The poor thing! Shut up indoors all the time, in deep mourning! She only goes out on Saturdays to confess and on Sunday mornings to take Communion, and then at Christmas and Easter, on the feast of the patron saint, and on All Souls' Day to go to the cemetery.'

'It seems to me she's got all the entertainment she needs, and then some. What more do you want, a brass band?'

Father Macaluso had difficulty restraining himself. 'You, moreover, are clearly not a good father.'

'Here we go again! What the hell have I got to do with it?'

'Oh, you've got plenty to do with it, damn it all!' said the priest, beginning to get worked up. 'You are never at home, but we all know where you are, and I even learned this morning that your sin will soon bear fruit. Are you not ashamed?'

'No, I'm not. I have no sense of shame. I follow nature.'

'Well, then, you should let your daughter follow nature, too, and in a more respectable manner.'

'And what would that be?'

'Marry her off.'

The marquis suddenly calmed down. The idea of being rid of 'Ntontò and clearing the way to bringing Trisina home with him could only appeal to him.

'She's never wanted to get married. And to think that she's had so many attractive offers.'

'But now it would be easy to persuade her. She's been left almost completely alone.'

'Have you got someone in mind?'

'Yes,' said the priest, but then he hesitated.

'Come on, out with it. What's his name?'

'Fofò La Matina. He's an honourable man, has no vices, doesn't drink, smoke, or gamble.'

'And every now and then he pops.'

'What do you mean?'

'Nothing,' said the marquis. Then, after a pause, he continued: 'Whose brilliant idea was this? Yours, 'Ntontò's, or the pharmacist's? Or all of you put together?'

'Your daughter and the pharmacist know nothing about this. It's something I and my dear friend Mrs Colajanni have been thinking about.'

'May I say something?'

'Of course.'

'You and your dear friend can put it you-know-where.'

Father Macaluso had made a vow, at the high altar, not to have it out with the marquis.

'Would you at least tell me what you have against the pharmacist?'

'I have nothing against the pharmacist. Actually, I rather admire the man. But he's got no social standing whatsoever. His father worked the land for my father. And you want me to give my daughter to the son of a clodhopper? Look, I've already forgotten what you said to me. Bring me someone of my daughter's station, and then we can talk.'

'Why, are you asking me to play matchmaker now?'

'Why not? After all, you're already wearing a dress.'

It turned into a shouting match.

Fifteen days before Trisina gave birth, Don Filippo grew very restless. He could not sit still for a minute, paced about the house lengthwise and widthwise, and didn't sleep a wink at night. He answered everyone rudely when addressed, and nothing worked the way he thought it should. One morning, as he was looking out of the window at his estate, he started shouting that the rows of vines were all crooked and needed to be set straight; another time he cursed the whole day long because the cock did not crow at a specific time of the morning, but whenever it suited him. The cock problem was serious.

'I have to go and talk to that shit of a cock,' he said to Natale. 'He wakes me up when he shouldn't, and when he should, he doesn't give a damn.'

'So, go and talk to him, then,' replied Natale, resigned.

The discussion between the marquis and the cock took place without the others knowing about it. They realized, however, that the cock had not budged from his intention to do things his way, since they found him with his neck broken.

One week before the expected date, the marquis went

into town and returned in the carriage with Mimì, followed by a farmhand with a caleche and the midwife, who had been paid her weight in gold. All the newborns of Vigàta who came into the world during her absence would have to make it on their own.

Fofò La Matina solemnly promised that he would come to Le Zubbie in three days. The little house was turned into a sort of campsite. The marquis slept in his own bedroom, the pharmacist in the room built for Natale, Maddalena – brought back just in case – in the press house, Mimì and the farmhand in the stable, Trisina and the midwife in the master bedroom, and Natale in a thatched hut in the vineyard within earshot.

When Trisina started yelling that her waters had broken, the multitude ran to her bedside. Only Natale and the marquis ran out of the house, sitting down on the stone wall of the well. They were teetering back and forth, like trees buffeted by the wind. And it wasn't clear whether it was a gesture of affection or precaution when the marquis put his arm around Natale. There was a stampede of people coming and going with pots of boiling water and clean cloths as Trisina screamed that she was breaking in two. Then a mysterious silence ensued, so complete that the two embracing men did not take a breath. It lasted an eternity. Pirrotta was staring at an ant climbing the stone wall, Don Filippo at a cricket that was cleaning itself.

They were roused from their stupor by the voice of the midwife, who was holding in one hand a sort of slaughtered, upside-down rabbit and shouting for joy: 'Come! It's a boy! It's a boy!'

Each supporting the other, the two men, gimpy-legged, stood up.

The day after the birth, the marquis wanted to give Fofò La Matina a lift into town with the caleche. After they had been travelling a while, the pharmacist broke the silence.

'Please forgive me, Marquis, but I feel obliged to tell you something.'

'Fire away,' said Don Filippo, who was in a good mood.

'You're no longer a young man. And you eat a lot. Your face is too ruddy. You should give it some thought.'

'What should I do?'

'I could apply some leeches, for preventive purposes.'

'Fofò, I prefer to have my blood sucked in other ways.'

'But, sometimes, when you've eaten a great deal, don't you feel a burning in the pit of your stomach?'

'Burning? I feel fire! Some nights Trisina spends hours making me gallons and gallons of bay-leaf infusion.'

'Bay-leaf infusion is only a palliative. With your permission, I will make you ten tablets. If you come by the pharmacy this afternoon, I'll have them ready for you. You should take one after each meal, if you've eaten a lot.'

After dropping off Fofò in Vigàta, the marquis continued on to the provincial capital and appeared at the home of Scimè the notary.

'Have you decided to make a will?' asked the notary, who was an old friend of his.

The marquis touched his balls dramatically.

'You know how it is, Scimè. I'm convinced that if I draw up a will, two days later I'll be in the graveyard. No, I came because I want to make a gift straightaway: all of Le Zubbie to a baby boy who was born yesterday. And then I want to adopt him.'

'As far as the gift is concerned, there's no problem. Adoption, however, is a complicated matter. I'll begin the paperwork tomorrow. But tell me something: who is this baby boy?'

'The son of my field watcher's wife.'

'All right, but where do you come in?'

'Oh, I come in, Scimè, believe me. I come in the same way the Holy Spirit came in.'

Returning to Vigàta, he went to see Papìa the accountant, took him to eat at an inn, and talked about business. He did not go home to see 'Ntontò.

After a while he dropped in at the pharmacy, picked up a little box of pills, and returned to Le Zubbie.

Pasta and sauce with chunks of sausage, suckling kid with potatoes, and a strange wine that Mimì had brought back and Trisina and Natale had never seen before. When the cork came out it made a pop so loud it sounded like a rifle shot. And it was treacherous: it went down as easy as water, but before long one's head was spinning. Such was the luncheon with which the marquis had wanted to celebrate the baby's first month of life.

When he had finished eating, Don Filippo said the meal was sitting a bit heavily on his stomach.

'Want me to go and get the pills, your excellency?' asked Trisina.

'No, Trisì. I think I'll go and lie down. If I fall asleep, wake me up at four.'

He brought a glass of water with him into his bedroom, took a pill from the little cardboard box he kept on his bedside table, swallowed it, and lay down.

When Trisina went to wake him at four, he was dead.

It was still dark outside when Mimì opened his eyes suddenly, hearing somebody pounding and kicking the great door and calling out wildly. He rolled out of bed, ran to open the door, and found Natale Pirrotta before him, pale and trembling as if he had malaria.

'What's going on?'

'The marquis . . . yesterday afternoon, after eating . . . he went out for a little walk . . . and we haven't seen him since . . . I've looked everywhere . . . but I can't find him.'

Mimì made a snap decision. He sent Natale off to

inform Inspector Portera while he himself, dressed as he was, went to shake the pharmacist out of bed.

Around midday one of Inspector Portera's men, who had ventured all the way to Vaso di Failla, a deep, desolate, funnel-shaped valley strewn with jagged rocks and crumbly, treacherous clay, with a few clumps of sorghum scattered here and there, fired a shot in the air to alert the others, who had spread out in several directions. The marquis's body lay at the bottom of the valley. When he arrived at the spot, Portera made everyone take a few steps back and started reading what the ground had to tell him. Then he called the others.

'The marquis slipped from here. See that streak right at the edge? The ground is naturally slippery there, so you can imagine what it would be like after the three days of rain we've had. Poor Don Filippo tried to stop his fall. See how that sorghum bush is stripped away? But it wasn't enough, and he kept on slipping. Then he must have gathered speed, probably broke his neck, and at the end of his fall even hit his head on a rock.'

'Why do you think he was already dead when he hit his head?' asked Fofò La Matina.

'Because there's very little blood on the rock. In any case, we'll know more after we bring in the body. But my question is: why did he venture so far from home, and to such a dangerous place?'

'The marquis, poor guy, wasn't all there in the head any more,' said Pirrotta.

'Oh, no?'

'It's true,' interjected the pharmacist. 'A few days ago Pirrotta told me the marquis broke a cock's neck because it didn't crow at the right time of day.'

Then he turned and addressed Pirrotta directly: 'Did the marquis eat a lot yesterday?'

'I'd told him not to; I'd warned him about eating so much. He must've fainted, or felt dizzy, and then he fell.'

'Well, let's be patient,' Portera concluded, 'and take him away.'

'May I ask a question?' enquired Fofò.

'Feel free.'

'Who should inform the daughter?'

There was silence. Nobody had the courage to volunteer.

'Well, if that's the way it is, I'll take care of it myself,' said the pharmacist. 'I'll go at once, so she'll be prepared when her father comes home dead.'

Portera was a born policeman. He sensed that something didn't add up in this affair, but couldn't work out what.

When the body was recovered from the valley, he sent it on to Vigàta with Mimì and dismissed his men. He brought his horse up alongside Pirrotta's mule. 'I want to see the room where the marquis slept.'

The first things he noticed on entering were the items

on the bedside table: a wallet, a leather pouch, and a small cardboard box. Don Filippo's gold watch had been found in his waistcoat pocket, still going, though the chain had been broken. The wallet was full of money, and the pouch filled with coins. Inside the little box he found four white pills.

'Do you know what these are?' he asked Trisina, who was nursing her baby.

'Yessir. Pills the pharmacist gave to his excellency. They helped the burning in his stomach.'

'I'm taking the wallet, pouch, and box with me.'

'As you wish, sir,' said Pirrotta.

The inspector sat down, poured himself a glass of wine without asking permission, and began questioning.

'Whose baby is that?'

'What do you mean, whose baby? He's mine,' said Pirrotta.

'Why was the marquis living here instead of at home?'

'We're not the ones you should be asking that. Maybe it's 'cause after his son died, he felt more comfortable living with us.'

'Why, didn't he feel comfortable at home?'

'Seems not. An' he felt so comfortable here, in fact, that he settled all the land in Le Zubbie on our son.'

The revelation hit the inspector like a blow to the stomach. The motive for a possible murder had just fallen away. Pirrotta felt no pity for him.

'And he wanted to adopt him. And me an' Trisina were in favour of it. And if you don't believe me, you can go ask Scimè the notary.'

'So, now that the marquis's dead, there's not going to be an adoption.'

'Nosir, no more adoption.'

'If it was up to us, the poor marquis, bless his soul, should've lived to be a hundred!' Trisina said, bursting into tears.

They waited for the sound of Portera's galloping horse to recede before beginning to talk. The baby had been put down to sleep, and they had a great many things to say.

'You were right,' said Trisina.

'Of course,' said Pirrotta. 'If they found 'im dead in the house, they would've sent us straight to San Vito prison. The law is always on the side of the nobles. As the proverb says: *Sauta un torzolu e va in culu all'ortolano* – "When a plant goes missing, it ends up in the gardener's arse."'

Without warning, Trisina felt a flash of warmth down below, a pang of desire that anticipated her first post-partum menstruation by a good ten days.

'Oh, Natale, my sweet Natale, love of my life!'

She jumped on his lap and started kissing his neck. And this time Pirrotta held her close.

*

'What are these pills in here?' the inspector asked, putting the little box on the counter in front of the pharmacist.

'Where did you find them?'

'On the marquis's bedside table at Le Zubbie.'

Fofò La Matina opened the box and looked inside. There were four pills left.

'I made these for the marquis, to alleviate his heartburn.'

'How many were there?'

'Ten.'

'Are you sure you didn't make a mistake?'

'As to the number?'

'No, not as to the number. As to what you prepared for him.'

The pharmacist's face hardened.

'I have never made a mistake in my life. And if you have any doubts, send those pills wherever you like and have them tested.'

'It hadn't even crossed my mind!' said the inspector, pocketing the little box.

(But of course it had crossed his mind, and he sent the pills to Palermo only to receive a negative response one month later. They consisted only of bicarbonate of soda and extracts of digestive herbs.)

The wake proceeded according to a specific ritual, which was, moreover, a timeworn tradition, since Palazzo Peluso had seen more than its share of deaths.

The marquis lay on the bed, a white band over his forehead to hide the wound. He looked as if he was dreaming, and his dream must have been beautiful, to judge by the smile on his face. Father Macaluso had arranged to have a rosary wrapped around the deceased's hands, but, for no apparent reason, every so often the rosary slipped out and onto the bed.

The women sat along the walls and prayed. The men, on the other hand, paid their last respects to Don Filippo, then withdrew to the salon to talk and smoke.

Every now and then Mimì and Peppinella went round offering the mourners rose liqueur and little pastries to boost their morale.

Around midday, 'Ntontò, who hadn't yet opened her mouth and whose eyes were dry but bewitched, rose without saying a word and left the room.

Fifteen minutes passed, then half an hour, and still 'Ntontò hadn't returned. At this point Mrs Colajanni, after exchanging a glance of understanding with the other women, went off to look for her. She was not in the salon with the men. Mrs Colajanni went into the kitchen, where Peppinella and Mimì were putting more pastries on trays.

'We haven't seen 'Ntontò for the last half hour,' she said.

Peppinella became immediately alarmed and rushed to the marchesina's room. 'Ntontò wasn't there, nor was she in the toilet. News of her disappearance quickly spread among the mourners, who started looking for her.

Baron Uccello had a sudden misgiving, which he expressed out loud: 'What if she decided to do what her grandfather did?'

The men all rushed out of the palazzo and spread out, some going into town, others taking the road to the harbour.

After finding no trace of 'Ntontò anywhere, however, they all returned to their respective homes, since it was time to eat. The women, too, after making one last sign of the cross in front of the deceased – who, as the hours passed, looked more and more like he was laughing – took their leave of Mimì and a weeping Peppinella. The only ones left in the palazzo were Father Macaluso – who cursed the saints as he prayed, because there was no one left to respond, the sacristan having taken advantage of the collective flight – and the pharmacist.

'Let's stay calm. We'll find her,' Fofò La Matina said after the others had left. He assigned the remaining party different areas to search. He himself went up to the attic. Mimì went to have a better look in the rooms checked earlier; Peppinella was sent to the stables, the storehouse, and the pantry on the ground floor of the palazzo. After opening some old cupboards and trunks, Fofò heard Peppinella yelling from below.

'Come down to the pantry! She's here!'

The pharmacist rushed downstairs. There in the pantry, perfectly calm, her skirt hitched up around her waist and her pants down, 'Ntontò was painting her bottom black.

Five

Barely two days after the marquis's funeral, Mrs Colajanni went to work on Father Macaluso.

'Does that seem right to you? Doesn't it cry out to God for vengeance that this child of sin is going to enjoy the vineyard of Le Zubbie? And that whore and her cuckolded pimp of a husband are going to live it up after killing poor Don Filippo?'

'Killing him? But the inspector said the marquis died after slipping and falling into the valley.'

'Yes, but why did he slip?'

'How should I know? He lost his footing.'

'No, sir. The pharmacist was like an open book on this point. He said that the marquis felt ill – he felt, I dunno, faint or something, and then he fell into the valley.'

'So?'

'You really surprise me, Father. He felt faint, or dizzy, because of the state that whore had left him in.'

'That whore, as you call her, and I'm sorry to defend her, did nothing more than what the marquis asked her to do. And anyway, I'm sorry, but what did they have to gain from Don Filippo's death? Had he lived, the marquis would have made them even richer.'

'No, no. Those two think the way peasants think. They decided that a bird in the hand – Le Zubbie today – was worth two in the bush.'

One thing led to another, and one night Father Macaluso came to a decision – not to prevent an injustice, but to commit one himself. By intervening in the matter, he would avenge himself of all the bad turns the marquis had done him.

The first thing he did was to go and see Papìa the accountant, who was an honourable man. Papìa confirmed the gift, but also pointed out that the marquis's possessions were so many and so vast that to lose Le Zubbie was like losing one drop from a bottle of wine. And his word was gospel: he had been Don Filippo's administrator and continued to perform the same service after Marchesina 'Ntontò had given him a vote of confidence. Father Macaluso pretended not to know any of this and turned up at the office of Scimè the notary.

'I don't understand by what right you are requesting this information of me,' the notary said coldly to him.

'By my rights as a citizen and priest,' Father Macaluso replied proudly.

'Rights which in this office are worth a pile of cowshit. In any case, just to dispel all doubt, I can tell you that this business of the gift is true, and that the legal heiress – the marchesina – has thirty more days to appeal it. But she had better find herself a good lawyer.'

'There aren't any surprises in store for us in the will, are there?'

'What will? Let me speak your tongue: it would have been easier to convince a camel to do that bullshit mentioned in the Gospel than to persuade the dear departed to draw up a will.'

Since he was already halfway there, Father Macaluso decided to go for broke and call on the lawyer Cassar, a luminary of his profession.

'We could try it,' the lawyer said, 'but we shall need more substantive arguments to prove the subject's mental incapacities.'

'What? Killing a cock because it didn't do what was asked of it, or screaming because the rows of vines weren't straight – aren't those the actions of a madman?'

'Not necessarily. Personally, for example, I happen to like my rows of vines nice and straight. And my mother kicks and curses at chairs that aren't where she wants them to be. And until proven otherwise, we are both of sound mind. Just let me handle this. Before we take another step, however, the marchesina must give her consent. She's the legal heir to everything.'

When Father Macaluso, in the company of Mrs Colajanni, went to talk about all this with the marchesina, 'Ntontò asked him a precise question.

'But why was my father so attached to that baby?'

To his genuine horror, Father Macaluso realized that 'Ntontò knew nothing, and that her naiveté had kept her from suspecting anything.

Madonna mia! thought the priest. Where to begin?

Mrs Colajanni came to his aid.

'The truth is the truth,' she proclaimed, 'and it should be shouted to the four winds because it offends neither mankind nor the Lord in heaven. Your father, my dear 'Ntontò, had been for some time shacked up with the field watcher's wife. That was why he was living at Le Zubbie. And everyone in town says the baby is his.'

'Ntontò didn't move, but only kept looking straight ahead, her eyes turning a brighter blue.

'And he gave Le Zubbie to him?'

'Precisely.'

'And he said he wanted to adopt him?'

'Precisely.'

'Ntontò stood up. The visit, for her, was over. 'Give me two days to think about it,' she said.

'What is there to think about?' Father Macaluso asked, screwing up his face.

'Two days. And thank you for your concern.'

✳

When 'Ntontò finished telling the pharmacist of the visit from Father Macaluso and Mrs Colajanni, he broke into a broad smile.

'You find it funny?' she said, slightly miffed.

'No, but I feel relieved. When Peppinella came to the shop to tell me you needed to see me, I thought you had fallen ill again. Luckily, that's not the problem.'

'I don't need to ask anyone's advice,' 'Ntontò said after explaining. 'I could ask Baron Uccello, but he's always taken my father's side. That's why I've come to you. You seem like an honest man. What's your opinion?'

'It's not easy to say,' said the pharmacist. 'In one sense, Father Macaluso is right. In the eyes of the townsfolk, that is.'

'If I based my decisions on what the townsfolk think, you wouldn't be here now, wasting your breath on me.'

'Right.'

'And so, before you give me your advice, I want to know how things went. First. You were summoned by my father to help the field watcher's wife. How did he behave? Pretend that you're answering the police inspector, not me.'

'He behaved as if he was the child's real father,' said Fofò, showing no doubt whatsoever. 'Then there was the matter of how they had rearranged the house. The field watcher no longer slept with his wife.'

'And my father did?'

'No, that's just it. They all slept apart, in different rooms.'

'Second. How did they treat my father?'

'In all honesty, both husband and wife were very fond of him.'

'Thank you,' said 'Ntontò, standing up. As the pharmacist was kissing her hand, she chided him: 'But you never gave me your advice.'

'Because I have never felt in a position to advise others. I can only speak for myself.'

'Then speak as if you were the marquis's son.'

'If my father had willed, not even in writing, but only by oral agreement, that all his belongings should go to whomsoever of his choosing, and I were left destitute and mad, I should not have raised a finger against his wishes. But I speak only for myself.'

'Thank you,' said 'Ntontò.

'Ntontò did not wait the two days she had requested to think things over. That evening, after speaking to Fofò La Matina, she sent Peppinella to Mrs Colajanni with a message. The note was only a few lines long, but that very brevity communicated the firmness of her decision. In essence, 'Ntontò said she would not sign any papers that went against her father's wishes, and she did not want to discuss the matter any further. In a fit of rage, Father Macaluso kicked his missal and sent it flying. The news spread at once and was received as more proof that the marchesina, since painting her bottom black, was not right in the head. Only one voice was raised in her defence. Indeed 'Ntontò received an enormous bouquet of roses with a card saying: 'To her father's true daughter.' It was signed 'Zizì', which was what 'Ntontò had called Baron Uccello since childhood. She replied with a note of thanks, inviting the baron to call on her at the palazzo whenever he wished.

Zizì did not wait to be asked twice. The following day he was sitting opposite 'Ntontò.

'I went to see your father twice at Le Zubbie,' said Baron Uccello. 'I missed him. I was used to seeing him every day. And so I took the carriage and left, intending to return to Vigàta that same evening. But, both times, he wouldn't listen to reason. I had to stay the night. I regretted this, because it was an imposition. Trisina had to vacate the room next to your father's for me, and went to sleep in Natale's bedroom, while Natale had to sleep in the stable.'

'And what did the two of you do?'

'We didn't do anything. Or rather, we did what we always did. We ate, we laughed, we played cards. Cards, you know, were the mirror of your father's soul. Did you know that, 'Ntontò?'

'No, Zizì. What do you mean?'

'I mean that when he was in good spirits and untroubled, there wasn't anyone he couldn't beat. But when something wasn't going right for him, he always lost. And those days at Le Zubbie, even if I had called upon God to intervene, I could never have won as much as one game. It drove me mad.'

'So he was happy.'

'Happy?' said the baron, thoughtful. 'He was in heaven, 'Ntontò.'

'This evening,' 'Ntontò said to Peppinella, 'I want you to lay the table for three.'

'Why, who's coming?' the maid asked, alarmed.

'Nobody's coming. From now on, I want you and Mimì to eat with me.'

'To sit at the same table as your excellency?!' Peppinella exclaimed, horrified.

'Why, have you got something against it?'

'Yes'm. First of all, iss not right. And second, me an' my husband got no table manners. I smack my lips, and Mimì unbuckles his trousers.'

'You can smack your lips as much as you like and unbuckle whatever you wish. I don't want any arguments.'

That evening, as she ate with Peppinella and Mimì, who sat still as two statues, 'Ntontò explained herself.

'If I keep eating alone I'll lose my mind.'

Then she turned to face the other two, looking them straight in the eyes.

'Do you, Peppinella, or your sister, Maddalena, or you, Mimì, do any of you know what my father was doing at Le Zubbie?'

'Yes,' said Mimì, barely audible.

'And why didn't you say anything to me?'

'Mimì wanted to tell you,' said Peppinella, 'but I said no. I didn't want your excellency to be sad.'

'With each passing day, the marchesina is showing every sign that she has inherited her father's lunacy,' Colajanni the postmaster said at the club. 'Now she's taken to eating at the same table as her servants! A noble!'

'Let's make a distinction,' said Baron Uccello. 'Those aren't ordinary servants. Peppinella and Mimì raised and groomed her.'

'So what? They're still servants.'

'And you're still a pile of shit,' Commander Aguglia, the ex-Garibaldino, calmly intervened.

Colajanni gasped for breath.

'What did you say? You shall answer for this!'

'Whenever and however you like. There's no danger in duelling with you. It's a well-known fact that, while shit may stink, it doesn't kill.'

'Consider yourself slapped.'

'I'll do nothing of the sort. Get up out of that chair and come and slap me in person. Which will lead to one of two things: either I'll give you such a kick in the arse that you'll fly all the way to Malta, or I'll wipe my face with a piece of paper the way I do my arse after I shit. The choice is yours.'

'Ntontò received another large bouquet of roses. The accompanying card said: 'For the lady who so bravely and scornfully put the Garibaldian ideal of equality into practice. Commander Aguglia'.

'What's he talking about?' 'Ntontò asked herself, puzzled.

Consternation, anger, and frowns coloured the faces of the majority of the townsfolk as the carriage with the Peluso coat of arms, with Mimì at the reins and Natale Pirrotta inside with Trisina holding the baby, entered Vigàta from Le Zubbie, crossed the Corso, and passed through the great door of the family palazzo. The minority, on the other hand – consisting in reality of only Baron Uccello and Commander Aguglia – rejoiced. And this without either side having a clue as to why they had come.

'The marchesina wanted to see them,' Mimì explained, to rid himself of two or three busybodies assailing him like rabid dogs. But he said nothing more, being himself in the dark as to the reason behind his lady's strange whim.

'*Madonna santa*, she's so beautiful!' Trisina thought upon seeing 'Ntontò, and the terror she had felt during the journey, dress clinging to her sweaty body and teeth tightly clenched, quickly passed. Unconsciously she was thinking that a woman who looked like the Blessed Virgin was incapable, by nature, of doing harm.

'I called you here,' 'Ntontò said to the group once they were gathered in the boudoir, 'because I wanted to see the baby.'

She approached Trisina's extended arms, parted the baby blanket, and gazed at the sleeping infant.

'He's beautiful,' she said after a pause. 'How old is he?'

'Three months.'

'Sit down.'

They all sat down, Natale and Trisina as stiff as brooms. 'I don't want to offend anybody. But I need to know. And I want to tell you straightaway that I myself do not feel offended by anyone: not by my father, not by you, much less by the baby.'

'Your excellency could never offend me. Just like the dear departed marquis never could,' said Pirrotta. 'Your excellency can ask me whatever she likes.'

'Whose is he?' asked 'Ntontò, gesturing at the baby.

'He's the dear departed marquis's,' said Pirrotta. 'An' I can hold my head high when I say it, 'cause there was no lying or betrayal. But people mustn't know this; for them, he's my son.'

'That's right,' said 'Ntontò, who had taken the baby from Trisina's arms and was now holding it.

'How did he die?' she asked after a pause.

'Peacefully, in his own bed. Without even realizing. When Trisina went in to wake him up, he was dead. And he didn't even look dead. He looked like he was sleeping,' said Pirrotta.

'And why did you throw him into a ravine?'

''Cause if they found him dead in our house, with all the gossip that's been going around in town, they would've said me and Trisina killed him. So I hoisted him onto my shoulders, I took him to the ravine, and made it so it'd look to Portera like the marquis slipped and fell.'

'Thank you for your sincerity.'

'Much obliged.'

'Ntontò rang the bell, and Peppinella came running, full of curiosity. Everything seemed calm.

'Peppinè, do me a favour. Go into my room and bring me the jewellery box that's on my chest of drawers.

'I did that for a reason,' she said to the others as soon as Peppinella had left. 'I could have gone and got it myself, but I want a witness. I don't want people to say that you stole what I want to give the baby.'

When the maid returned, 'Ntontò opened the inlaid box and extracted a small, solid-gold chain with a medallion bearing a cameo of the marquis's profile.

'My father had this made for me,' she said, putting the chain around the baby's neck.

Natale knelt down, took his mistress's hand, and covered it with kisses and tears.

'And for whatever else you may need,' said 'Ntontò, 'I'm here for you.'

The news that the Marchesina Antonietta Peluso di Torre Venerina had been left the sole surviving member of her family reached the ears of a certain Baron Nenè Impiduglia by chance, after a delay of a few months. And it was the eldest son of Baron Uccello who told him, at a reception at the Officers' Club of Palermo. Hearing the catalogue of 'Ntontò's misfortunes, Nenè Impiduglia made a public display of his emotions.

'First thing tomorrow, I'm leaving for Vigàta,' he announced.

And he kept his promise. When he disembarked from the *Franceschiello*, however, his arrival sparked no curiosity. Actually, it was, in a certain sense, expected.

'The hunter has arrived,' was, in fact, Baron Uccello's only comment.

Nenè had long been known in town for his frequent visits to his 'dear auntie', Donna Matilde, who had been a mother to him for a while after his parents left the world of the living when their carriage overturned. The visits were brief, lasting only as long as it took for the mail boat to moor and unmoor again. But he would return to Palermo with his arms full. Indeed, the general chorus in town, when people saw Nenè arrive, was always: 'Nenè has come to load up.'

'What does your nephew do in Palermo?' people would ask the marchesa.

'He studies mathematics,' Donna Matilde would reply. And it was true. Nenè studied the numerical permutations of the roulette wheel with dogged devotion, and this long, assiduous course of study relieved him of vast sums of money. And so, to prevent his studies from being interrupted by a lack of funds, every so often Impiduglia would show up in Vigàta to visit his aunt, who would generously refill his coffers.

This time Nenè did not sleep at the palazzo, as he had always done. After informing his cousin that he had arrived, and requesting a visit, he took a room at the inn. The following morning, dressed all in black, he went to the cemetery to pray at the noble family vault of the Pelusos. He stayed for an hour, glued to the spot.

'He cried and cried,' the sexton later recounted. 'In fact, he cried so much, I had to give 'im a handkerchief 'cause 'is own was all soaked.'

After the cemetery he went into the church and left a bag of coins with Father Macaluso so the priest would say Masses for the salvation of the blessed souls of the departed.

'Especially for Donna Matilde,' he recommended.

'He's a good man, you have to admit,' said Baron Uccello

when he was told of Nenè Impiduglia's morning activities. 'I think he may just succeed in bagging 'Ntontò.'

'Ntontò had invited her cousin to lunch, but Impiduglia did not turn up. In his stead, he sent a signed note in which he wrote that he had been too deeply affected by his visit to the cemetery and therefore did not feel up to the engagement. Could they perhaps postpone the invitation until suppertime?

The moment Impiduglia saw 'Ntontò, his heart leapt, as when a carriage wheel dips into a hole in the road.

'Death becomes her,' he thought as he eyed her. She was like a ray of sunlight. At once his eyes turned into fountains. They embraced. And suddenly a scene from many years before came back to 'Ntontò, the time she and Nenè had hidden in the attic and her cousin had taught her a new game called 'doctor', where he had her lie down on an old sofa, raised her little skirt, and examined her tummy and the area round about at length. With a sense of shame, she felt the same flash of heat she had felt then.

They ate in silence. It was clear that Nenè was devastated and didn't feel like talking. In fact, they didn't even get to the second course. He stood up, kissed his cousin's hand, and ran off.

'He's too sensitive,' said 'Ntontò, recounting the evening to Mrs Colajanni and Signora Clelia, who had paid her a call.

'And good-looking, too,' said Signora Clelia, who, upon first seeing him a few days before, had judged his capacities.

'So what will he do? Isn't he going to come back?' asked Mrs Colajanni.

'He's coming back next week. He had to rush back to Palermo to return to his mathematics studies.'

'He must have a big head,' said Signora Clelia, without explaining what she meant.

Exactly one week later, Nenè returned to Vigàta.

'Let's see what the hell he's cooked up this time,' said Baron Uccello.

He had cooked up something good. A crate was unloaded from the *Franceschiello* and directly delivered, at Nenè's behest, to the church.

'The last time, when I came to have the Masses said for the dear departed,' he explained to Father Macaluso, 'I noticed that the altar was bare. Allow me to make a gift.'

And from the crate emerged a statue of St Anthony that looked alive, with the prettiest of faces and eyes upturned to heaven.

Upon seeing the gift, the priest decided that Nenè Impiduglia had all the qualities of sainthood.

For the next four months, Nenè proceeded to go back and forth between Palermo and Vigàta, and when 'Ntontò seemed sufficiently softened up, he declared his intentions.

He knew that, for a variety of reasons, Father Macaluso, Mrs Colajanni, and Signora Clelia were on his side.
As were Peppinella and Mimì, since not a day went by in
which he didn't slip them some money. The two servants,
however, didn't do it only for money; they were old and
worried about their mistress's future.

'Have people told you anything about me?' he asked
'Ntontò.

'Nothing at all. What would they have told me?'

'Oh, they'll tell you, all right. They'll tell you, for
example, that I've put all the money I had into my math-
ematical researches.'

'But I already know that.'

'Yes, but if you accept the proposal I am about to
make you, everyone in town will say I'm doing it for one
purpose only: to get my hands on your money. And it's
not true, 'Ntontò, I swear it, on your mother's soul, it's not
true.'

'And what is this proposal you want to make?'

''Ntontò, shall we bring our two lonely lives together?
No, don't answer just yet. I'll come back in a few days,
same time as today. I shall hope to find your front door
still open—'

A histrionic sob cut his last word short.

In the three days that followed, 'Ntontò had no peace.
The first to arrive was Father Macaluso.

'He's a lad of noble sentiments. An ideal father of a family. And it is your duty, Marchesina, to marry. When your dear departed father was still alive, I told him it was time you found a husband. He said he agreed, so long as your future spouse was of equal standing. And it appears to me that Baron Nenè Impiduglia holds all the cards in that regard. So you should respect your father's wishes.'

'When it's convenient, you mean?' 'Ntontò asked with a wry smile. She was referring to the adoption of Trisina's baby, which the priest had fought tooth and nail to thwart. But Father Macaluso failed to grasp her subtlety.

The second person to call on her was Mrs Colajanni.

'Let us speak woman to woman. You, 'Ntontò, after all the torments you've been through, are no longer the same. You need a man with a good head on his shoulders beside you, a man who will be both a husband and a father to you. Impiduglia is that man.'

The third person was Signora Clelia.

'Let us speak woman to woman. You are a virgin, 'Ntontò, and you don't know what you are missing. A real woman needs a man. There is nothing more beautiful than when a man and a woman embrace. You cannot die without having experienced this.'

Entirely unexpectedly, Papìa the accountant also showed up. 'I've heard the talk about town, and so I decided to come and see you on my own. Do you know, Marchesina, how old I am?'

'In your seventies?' said 'Ntontò.

'Yes, that's right. And my head's not what it used to be. More and more these days, I can't do my numbers, and my eyes go all foggy. If you, your excellency, get married and your husband takes over the administration of your estate, I can retire in peace. Think it over.'

Before the three days were up, 'Ntontò sent for Fofò La Matina.

'What should I do?' she asked him after telling him all that had been happening.

And Fofò told her, dispassionately, what she should do. The following day he was accosted by Baron Uccello.

'So you're with the rest of them, trying to fuck the quail?' said the baron.

'I'm not trying to fuck anyone. But I didn't feel like telling the marchesina she should die of loneliness and melancholy.'

Still on the subject of loneliness, Nenè Impiduglia, once he had received 'Ntontò's affirmative reply, headed back to Palermo with a purse full of money he had had Papìa advance him on the marchesina's dowry. He gambled half of it and lost, as was the general rule, but with the other half he began to set things right. He sold the little house he had in the city, and the proceeds equalled what was left of Papìa's money. He paid off fifteen creditors who very nearly died of surprise, and then he got down to the most serious business at hand — that is, dumping his two mistresses. With the first, Tuzza, the daughter of a man who sold vegetables in the streets, it was a simple matter.

'How much would it cost for you to buzz off?'

Tuzza spat out a figure. They spent the entire afternoon bargaining, then ate and spent the night fucking. The following morning they reached an agreement.

With his second mistress, Jeannette Lafleur, aged thirty, a leading lady at the theatre – known as Gesualda Fichera in the real world – things were a bit more complicated. Jeannette had a flair for the dramatic, like all women of the stage, and claimed she was in love with Nenè. It was not a question of money.

'I missed you like the very air I breathe,' she would say to Nenè whenever he returned after a few days' absence. And there was always hell to pay, because before Impiduglia could get down to the business of having sex with her, he had to listen to an endless litany of gossip about how the supporting actress was a slut who was corrupting the innocent soul of the young male lead, and the theatre manager didn't go a day without making lewd propositions to her, and the prompter had pretended to be distracted during the climactic scene and left her helpless on the stage, feeling utterly at sea on a ship sailed by pirates. After which Jeannette, tired from talking so much, would turn towards the wall and offer him, at last, the perfect shape of her back.

'I've been unwell,' Nenè said upon returning from Vigàta.

'Unwell in what way?' Jeannette asked.

'Oh, I don't know. I fainted three times.'

'Why don't you see a doctor?'

The following evening, as soon as Jeannette turned towards the wall, Nenè said: 'I'm sorry, darling, I'm not up to it. I can't do it. This morning, the doctor, after examining me, made a strange face. He wants me to come back tomorrow.'

Immediately assuming the role of the generous nurse, Jeannette hugged and kissed him all night.

The next day, as Jeannette was making herself up in her dressing room, the door flew open to reveal Nenè. A dead man standing on his own two feet by a miracle. His suit was all rumpled, his hair dishevelled, his tie crooked. He was looked pale, as if all the blood had been drained from his body. He collapsed into a chair and said in a faint, barely audible voice:

'Please, Jeannette, a glass of water.'

The theatre manager arrived at once with a glass.

'Jeannette,' said Nenè, 'the doctor has spoken: I've got two months left to live, give or take a few days. Try to be brave.'

Jeannette started trembling, and the manager had her drink the remaining water in the glass.

'Our love story ends here,' Nenè resumed, with some

effort. 'I don't want to be a burden to you. You have your life, your career. This is where I make my exit. But you, you've got to grit your teeth: the show must go on.'

Jeannette realized that at this point in the script she was supposed to scream and then faint. Which she did. After entrusting Jeannette to the seamstress, the manager helped Nenè to his feet and accompanied him with difficulty to the exit.

'Shall I call a cab, Baron?'

Nenè looked at him, smiled, and straightened up. 'No thanks, I can walk.'

And he set off at a brisk pace. A moment later, the manager caught up to him.

'Was that all an act?'

'Of course.'

'How much do you want?'

'For what?'

'To sign up with my company. You knock the spots off the best actors I know.'

While Nenè was taking care of business in Palermo, Father Macaluso and Mrs Colajanni were holding a council.

'There are a few hitches,' the priest began. 'Baron Nenè and the marchesina are first cousins. They're going to need a dispensation in order to marry.'

'And who would grant that?'

'The bishop.'

'So go and talk to the bishop, then.'

'But that's not the only thing. There's also the problem of deep mourning. Because if strictly observed, there's no question of marriage for quite a while yet.'

'But can't the bishop take care of that, too?'

'Yes, of course. But I've done some maths. Between one thing and another, a grandfather, a brother, a mother, and a father have died. In simple words, 'Ntontò is supposed to be holed up at home for at least nine years. Talk about marriage!'

'But nobody can survive nine years of engagement!'

'Exactly. We must find a solution. Tomorrow I'm going to talk to the bishop's secretary, Monsignor Curtò, who is a reasonable man.'

Monsignor Curtò discussed the matter with the bishop and, less than a week later, Father Macaluso was summoned to the diocesan curia.

'Concerning the matter of cousinship,' began the bishop, who was a man of scarce words and concrete acts, 'there is no problem. It's all up to me and can be easily resolved. The question of mourning, however, is not my province. It is God's.'

'So how will we negotiate with God?'

The bishop smiled; he had always appreciated Father Macaluso's wit.

'Don't you know that we are His intermediaries on

earth? You are one, and I, in all modesty, am another. Thus, my son, you should know that some of the dead are good, and some are bad. In our case, the elder marquis and the younger marquis are bad, very bad. They passed away in a state of mortal sin, one by committing suicide, and the other while he was committing adultery. I can shorten the nine years of mourning to thirty-six months. More than that I cannot do. But there are certain rules that must be respected. Monsignor Curtò has prepared the tally.'

The tally ended up amounting to two Masses a week for each of the two marquises, and one weekly Mass each for Donna Matilde and her son, said Masses to be held, of course, over the thirty-six-month period. In addition there were certain offerings to be made to charitable institutions such as the Pauper's Table and the Orphans of St Theresa and so on. The total amount of these offerings was to be disbursed in one single settlement to Monsignor Curtò, who would see to their fair distribution. When all was said and done, an arm and a leg. The banns would be published, in church and at the town hall, when the thirty-six months were over.

'But, where I come from, thirty-six months means three years!' Nenè snapped, when he was told the conditions imposed by the bishop.

'Where I come from, too,' said Father Macaluso. 'But think about it for a minute. First of all, it means three years starting from the last death – that is, the marquis's.

Well, a good eight months have passed since that sad day. Which means that you must wait two years and four months. Got that? All it takes is a little patience. You, in the meantime, should set yourself up in Vigàta, go calmly about your business, and get to know 'Ntontò a little better. You can even continue your studies of mathematics.'

'They haven't got the proper equipment here,' said Impiduglia. Then he added: 'And where's all the money for the Masses and offerings going to come from?'

It came from 'Ntontò. After all, the dead were hers. Signora Clelia, moreover, did her part to help Nenè Impiduglia pass the time during his long wait. She had him rent a small flat that had just been vacated across the landing from her own.

In the two years that followed, two things happened.

First, one Sunday, when he was eating at the home of his fiancée, Nenè Impiduglia stopped speaking in the middle of a sentence, turned pale, and dropped his face slowly into his soup. Brought to the provincial capital for an examination, he was found to be diabetic.

The second thing that happened was that 'Ntontò had a white border sewn onto the hems of her blouses and skirts, a sign that a ray of light was beginning to shine through the blackness.

Six

With only three months to go before the banns were published, Nenè Impiduglia was like a castaway at sea who, breathing his last, can finally see land. And at that moment, the steamship *Pannonia*, the most luxurious of the Sicilian and International Line, having sailed from New York, docked in the harbour of Palermo. Among the many passengers to disembark was a gentleman of about fifty who spoke pure Sicilian and had an American wife. With a great load of luggage in train, he took a suite at the Hotel des Palmes, where only the rich went to stay. For the time being, not a soul knew of his arrival, which would upset not only Nenè Impiduglia's plans, but the entire town of Vigàta.

They were talking about what sort of wedding it should be, who to invite, and whether it should be a great celebration or only a family affair, when Peppinella came in with an envelope in her hand.

'This just arrived on the *Franceschiello*, from Palermo.'

The arrival of a letter was an unusual event, and 'Ntontò wasted no time opening it. Upon reading it, she only had time to cry, 'Uncle Totò!' before fainting. As Nenè busied himself trying to revive her, he asked himself, 'Who the hell is Uncle Totò?'

'Any story worthy of respect (and which respects itself first and foremost, before demanding the respect of others) always begins twenty years earlier,' Baron Uccello said at the club, immediately falling speechless in shock, for never had he uttered words so rich and profound. Taking comfort, he resumed his tale.

Salvatore Maria Peluso di Torre Venerina was a year younger than his brother, Don Filippo. But the distance between the two, in their ways of thinking and living, was greater than that separating the earth and the moon. Don Filippo was a jocund spirit, always laughing and enjoying life to the fullest, always drinking, eating, and chasing women. Don Salvatore instead spent his life in the company of books, to the point that he had even started wearing spectacles. When they were growing up, a day never passed without them coming to blows over the silliest trifles. Later the arguments between Don Filippo and Don Totò became more serious, even if they no longer raised their fists. The new cause for squabbling was politics, Don Totò being a Bourbon royalist and Don Filippo a firm supporter of Italian unity. By the end of 1860, Don Totò disappeared from Vigàta.

'He's gone to Calabria, to be with the bandits,' Don Filippo used to say. And by calling the thirty thousand rebels in those parts 'bandits', he was subscribing to the hasty, vague definition given them by the Piedmontese. Then, somehow, it came to be known that Don Totò had placed himself under the command of General Borjes, the Spaniard sent to lead the Bourbon troops. When Borjes and his general staff were shot at Tagliacozzo without a trial, the name of Salvatore Peluso did not figure among those executed by the Bersaglieri. Through indirect channels, Don Filippo came to learn that his brother had managed to escape to America. And since that time he had no more news of him. Finally, after some ten years had passed, he believed him dead.

Instead he was alive and kicking and ready to set foot back in Vigàta. Rumours about town said that he was so rich that if he loaded all his money onto the *Franceschiello*, she would sink to the bottom from the weight. They also said that Don Totò's American wife was called Harriet and had the look and bearing of a wife, and that they had brought with them a secretary named Petru, a Calabrian by birth and a friend of Don Totò's since the days when they fought together with the bandits, as well as an elderly woman as black as night who went by the name of Nettie and was a sort of cook and maid.

On the day long awaited by all, four carriages pulled up in front of the wide open door of Palazzo Peluso. All of Vigàta was at the window or in the piazza, looking on. It was like the patron saint's feast day.

Out of the first carriage stepped Don Totò, tall, erect, and bespectacled, his face so marked by wrinkles and scars that it looked like a sea chart, and his wife Harriet, a sort of beanpole with no tits or hips and sallow skin. From the second coach emerged Petru, he, too, about fifty years old, small of stature and thin, looking around, his little head turning left and right like a ferret's. Out of the third carriage stepped the black maid, fat and old and with two eyes so big they looked like portholes on a steamship. Little children began to cry at the sight of her. The last carriage was full of luggage, which Mimì and Peppinella hoisted onto their shoulders and carried inside. Then the door shut behind them, and the celebration, for the moment, was over.

Uncle Totò spared his niece the task of recounting the family's misfortunes. For reasons unclear, he already knew everything, even about the baby his brother had sired with Trisina.

'Tomorrow we shall all go to the cemetery to see them,' said 'Ntontò.

'Why?' asked Uncle Totò, looking at her in astonishment. 'The dead are dead, after all.'

Then, after a pause, he continued: 'Have you still got Curcunella?'

'Ntontò sprang to her feet, left the room, and returned with a doll, a baby doll her uncle had given her when she wasn't yet three years old. Curcunella was the name they had given her, and she had remained a secret between them.

'Here she is.'

Uncle Totò took the doll into his hands, while 'Ntontò, who until that moment had managed to hold back, broke out in tears.

'Come here,' said her uncle.

He sat her down beside him on the sofa, put an arm around her shoulders, and 'Ntontò quite naturally laid her head on his chest.

But then the door suddenly flew open. It was Peppinella, trembling and shouting:

'I won't work in the same kitchen as that black thing!'

'Ntontò quickly found a solution.

'Let's do this: you cook in the other kitchen for yourself and Mimì, and Nettie will cook for the rest of us.'

'And what about tonight?'

'What you mean, "tonight"?'

'I mean that that black thing has put her baggage in the room next to ours.'

'But what are you afraid of? Haven't you got Mimì sleeping beside you?'

'Mimì don't like the look of this, either.'

Nettie, the 'black thing', was asked to move her luggage upstairs. She would sleep in the master's wing.

That afternoon, Baron Uccello asked if he could pay a call.

He and Don Totò threw themselves into each other's arms, and then immediately locked themselves in the little room where the late Don Filippo had his office. Totò offered the baron a cigar as big as a stovepipe.

'So why did you let us think you were dead?'

'That wasn't me. It was my brother who became convinced of it.'

'All right, but you went twenty whole years without giving any sign of life!'

'Well, for the first few years I couldn't afford to send news. When I arrived in America with Petru, the war between the North and the South was on. I was on the side of the South, and took part in the Battle of Chattanooga. In fact our commander, General Lee, made me a colonel. Then I met Harriet, whose father owned some cotton fields, and we got married. I have two children, a boy and a girl, named Federico and Matilde, like my father and mother. At the moment they're with their grandmother, Harriet's mother. Then I moved to a place called Texas and bought myself a well. And I made some money.'

'With a well?'

'An oil well, Baron, not a water well.'

'All right, but why, after the war, when you got married and made all that money, did you never drop me a line?'

'What would have been the use? I would have had to write a whole novel, and nobody would have believed it.'

'Will you be staying long in Vigàta?'

'A few months. Then I shall go back to America. But while I've got you here, I'd like to ask you something. 'Ntontò told me she's engaged to a cousin I can't remember, Nenè Impiduglia. Do you know him?'

'My children, who live in Palermo, know him well. They also know he's made his share of mischief in his day.'

'Oh, really?'

'Really.'

And the baron told him what he had to tell him.

In the week that followed, Petru proved his worth.

On his boss's behalf, he bought the columned house that the 'Anglo Sulphur Company' had put up for sale, then brought in a caravan of craftsmen to set it completely right, paying what he had to pay.

'Why, is there not enough room in the marchesa's palazzo?' people asked about town.

'Don Totò doesn't want to put them out.'

Then Petru went off to Palermo to load onto the *Franceschiello* some more trunks that had arrived from America. In Vigàta, Sasà Mangione and three cronies were hired to unload them and arrange their contents in the proper places inside the house, and they worked for four days. When it was all over, Sasà pocketed a silver snuff box. In twenty days' time, the house was ready to be inhabited, and Don Totò and his wife, secretary, and black house-keeper moved into their new home. Don Totò then went and spoke to the president of the Sicilian Credit and Discount Bank.

'What's wrong? You look pale,' the postmaster said to the president when he appeared at the club that evening.

'Never mind,' said the banker.

'Come on, what happened? What is it?'

'What happened is that this morning Don Totò requested that a portion – a very small portion – of the money he deposited in Palermo should be transferred to me.'

'So?'

'So, there are so many zeroes in that account, they stretch from here to the harbour wall. Which gave me a terrible headache.'

After taking care of what needed to be done, Petru went back to Palermo to see to a delicate matter that Don Totò had told him about.

Meanwhile, the daily morning farce began for the people of Vigàta. This consisted of Nettie the maid going out shopping while not understanding a word of Sicilian, which always resulted in total confusion. The entertainment didn't last long, however, because that friend to foreigners, Fede the surveyor, soon came to her aid. There was one thing Nettie was insistent about, however, and that was going to the pharmacy and asking for the strangest things. One day, for example, she wanted a pair of socks.

'She says you can do that in her country,' explained Fede the surveyor, who spoke a smattering of English. 'She says you can buy everything at the pharmacy, which she calls a store.'

Thus, every so often, Fofò La Matina, just to make her happy, would sell her something.

Don Totò had got into the habit of frequenting the club, and whenever he entered, he was immediately surrounded. Fede the surveyor was particularly good at egging him on, getting him to tell stories about America compared to which the puppet theatre and the tales of the paladins of France seemed like small potatoes. There wasn't a day, however, when the marquis – since the title now fell to him – failed to pay a call upon his niece.

To Nenè Impiduglia he was aloof; just 'Good morning' and 'Good evening'. 'Ntontò had noticed her uncle's behaviour towards her fiancé, but didn't have the courage to ask him about it.

Some ten days before the banns were published, as 'Ntontò was getting ready to change into the clothes for half-mourning, Petru came in from Palermo on the mail boat.

'It's all here,' he said, putting a large envelope on his boss's desk. 'Looks like some stormy weather's on the way.'

The marquis opened the envelope and started reading the documents.

'So, what have you decided?' Baron Uccello asked him later at the club. 'Will you stay in Vigàta or go back to America?'

'I'm going to stay a few more days, settle some business, and then go back to America. I don't want to die here.'

'Aren't you going to wait until your niece's wedding?'

The marquis looked at him and said nothing. As for the place of his death, however, he turned out to be a bad prophet.

Entering Don Totò's office-chamber, Father Macaluso noticed that Baron Uccello was already there, and he was none too pleased about this. Whatever the reason for Petru summoning him, he knew that the baron would not be neutral. Uccello could never stand priests.

The marquis rose, came up to greet him, held out his hand, and invited him to sit down.

'Can I get you anything?'

'No thank you, Marquis, at this hour it would ruin my appetite.'

'Then I'll get straight to the point. I took the liberty of disturbing you, dear Father, because I know it was you who persuaded my niece to become engaged to Impiduglia.'

'Good God, it wasn't only me. There were also Mrs—'

'I don't care about the ladies involved.'

'Well, even the pharmacist—'

'Never mind the pharmacist. And don't keep back-pedalling, or you're likely to fall and hurt yourself. You know what I mean?'

'Yes, of course.'

'Since 'Ntontò has already suffered a great deal, I, as her uncle, must make certain she doesn't suffer more and worse.'

'What could be worse than losing her parents and brother?'

'There are worse things, I assure you, Father. At any rate, I sent Petru to Palermo to find out about this Impiduglia. Let us begin by saying that he has had four mistresses.'

Father Macaluso smiled.

'Do you find that amusing?'

'No, these are things young people do. But since Impiduglia has been living in Vigàta, he has definitely put himself back on the right path.'

'What path? The path into Clelia Tumminello's bed?'

Father Macaluso stopped smiling.

'Let us now turn to more serious matters. Impiduglia is

a hardened gambler. It's a disease for him. He has lost his entire inheritance playing cards and roulette.'

'I didn't know that.'

'I'm sure you didn't. And you want to know something else? He had Papìa advance him part of 'Ntontò's dowry, then immediately gambled half of it away. But that's not all. He has already been convicted twice for fraud. Have a look at these documents.'

Father Macaluso approached the small stack of papers on the desk. These weren't rumours: they were extracts of verdicts and sworn declarations.

'What should I do?' he asked, resigned.

'You must talk to Impiduglia. I will give him three days to think things over, because I am offering three options. The first is that he leaves and goes wherever the hell he pleases, and sends 'Ntontò a nice letter saying that he no longer feels like being tied down, that he's not the marrying kind. The second is that he doesn't leave, and the war begins. In this case I will become my niece's guardian, forbid him to see her, and the only way Baron Impiduglia will ever see any of 'Ntontò's money is through a telescope. I won't have any problem obtaining such authorization from the courts. The law always follows the path that money tells it to follow. The third is that he comes here, to my house, asks me to forgive him for wishing to harm 'Ntontò, I give him a little money as a parting gift, and we all go our merry ways with God's blessing. But he must not make any mistakes, such as trying to see 'Ntontò during these three days. Send him word that she doesn't feel well.'

'I'll tell him,' said the priest, standing up. Before leaving, however, he had a question.

'Could you tell me what right Baron Uccello had to be present at this meeting?'

'He's a witness. I wouldn't want the things I have said to be distorted after we leave this room. And, while we're on the subject of rights, if you want to say a comforting word to your protégé, tell him that the only right entitling him to marry 'Ntontò was the fact that he's a noble.'

It took less than four hours for all of Vigàta – except for 'Ntontò – to learn what sort of person Nenè Impiduglia was and to hear about the scene that had taken place between Don Totò and Father Macaluso. The only person to benefit from Nenè's staying at home was Signora Clelia.

'But is it true you were convicted?'

'Yes.'

'Let's do it again. Ahh, God, that's good! Again! No, wait, Nenè, now let's do it this way.'

When the three days were up, a hundred eyes followed Impiduglia's every step as he walked from his flat to the house with the columns. Night was falling.

Looking into the eyes of the marquis, who was sitting behind his desk, Nenè got scared. Those were the eyes – he was sure of it – of a man who had killed, perhaps even in cold blood. He opened his mouth to speak but it felt walled up.

'Water,' he managed to say.

The marquis did not budge, but kept eyeing him like a snake about to eat a mouse. Nenè turned his back and followed a smell of rabbit cacciatore down a corridor until he reached the kitchen. Nettie wasn't there. Resting on the windowsill was a sweating jug of water. He picked it up and drank it. Having done what he needed to do, he returned to the office.

'I've come to tell you I accept your third offer.'

Without taking his eyes off him, Don Totò opened a drawer, extracted a fat envelope, and tossed it near Nenè's hands.

'In America,' he said, 'I would have spared myself the expense. You should thank God we're not in America.'

Nenè put the envelope in his pocket. 'And who's going to tell 'Ntontò?'

'I'll take care of that. Don't you worry about it.'

Impiduglia turned on his heel and left. Don Totò wiped his face with his hand, sighing deeply, and rang the bell.

'It's all over, Petru,' he said to his secretary as soon as he appeared. 'He took the money. And we could not have expected otherwise, given the character of this shit of a man. Do me a favour: go to 'Ntontò and tell her I'm coming to lunch tomorrow.'

'Will the missus also come?'

'No, Harriet gets bored. She can't understand a word we say. This journey has been hard on her. But in a few days we're going back to America.'

'Ntontò waited until past two o'clock for her uncle to come to the palazzo. Then, seeing that he still had not arrived, she began to get nervous. She understood that Don Totò, in inviting himself to lunch, wanted to talk about Nenè and explain the reason for his behaviour. She rejected Peppinella's advice to sit down in the meanwhile and begin eating; instead she decided to send Mimì to the house with the columns to find out what the problem was.

Mimì knocked on the door of Don Totò's house, but nobody answered. Two things made him immediately suspicious: the first was that, though it was afternoon, he could see a lamp burning in one of the windows; and second, there was a smell of burnt meat coming from under the front door.

At once he ran to alert Inspector Portera, who wasted no time having his assistant break down the door. And the scene that greeted the inspector, his man, and Mimì was such that the three simultaneously took off their hats. They felt as if they had entered a wax museum.

Sitting at a round table impeccably set for dinner, Don Totò was raising a forkful of spaghetti to his mouth, Harriet was wiping her lips with her napkin, and Petru was reaching for a slice of bread with his right hand. In the kitchen Nettie was also sitting, with a plate on her knees and looking at a cooker, now extinguished, upon which sat a pan with a completely charred rabbit cacciatore in it. There was no sign of violence. It was a perfect picture of everyday life. One almost expected these people, surprised at an intimate moment, to stand up and demand an explanation for the intrusion. Portera had seen many murders over the years, some of them frighteningly imaginative, but here it was the very lack of violence, or the apparent lack, that turned his stomach. His first thought was that it must have been a mistake by the black maid. It was well known that Nettie was obsessed with flavouring her spaghetti with the first things that came to mind. Then, all at once, the inspector remembered what the townsfolk had said about Don Totò and Nenè Impiduglia.

Soon many people, after learning that the dead looked like statues, wanted to visit the museum. Frightened at the prospect, Portera sent for Lieutenant Baldovino and a small contingent of soldiers. The lieutenant tightened the knot around Impiduglia's neck.

'I saw Mr Impiduglia last night, right here in this house. He was near the kitchen window, drinking water.'

Nenè, therefore, had somehow managed to enter the kitchen, where it would have been easy for him to put poison in the pot of water boiling for the spaghetti. The motive for vendetta was well established, and everyone knew it.

Portera and two of his men dashed off to the house where Nenè had been staying. They knocked on the door, but it was Clelia's door, across the landing, that opened.

'What is it? What do you want? Mr Impiduglia left early this morning. For Palermo. He said he was going to resume his studies.'

'Break down the door,' Portera ordered his men.

'But there's no need!' Signora Clelia intervened. 'He left me the key to give back to the landlord, and he also left me the rent money.'

Her last statement slightly ruffled the inspector. Why would someone who has just finished killing four people bother to return their key and pay the rent? But the thought quickly faded from his mind when he saw the disorder of Nenè's flat, with everything turned upside down, the sign of a hasty departure.

Had he asked Signora Clelia, he would have learned that the disorder in that apartment was the normal order of Nenè Impiduglia's life.

Rediscovering the poker face of his former life as a brigand, Mimì told his mistress that Don Totò had had to go to the provincial capital for some important business. The marquis would come to lunch the following day. Having set 'Ntontò's mind at rest with this whopper, he went to the shop, told the pharmacist what had happened – which

Fofò, of course, already knew – and asked him to tell his mistress everything. He himself didn't feel up to it.

Fofò replied that he would take care of it, but that in the meantime, Mimì should tell the marchesina that he would drop by in the evening.

'And you, Father, don't know which of Don Totò's three offers Impiduglia was ready to accept?' asked Portera.

'No, I don't,' said Father Macaluso. 'I merely communicated to him what the marquis had told me.'

'But what are you trying to discover?!' Baron Uccello butted in. 'He killed them, it's as simple as that! He had it all planned. It's possible he was going to accept one of the three offers – in my opinion the third, where he would take the money and leave – but then hatred made him change his mind.'

'We'll know the answer when we find him,' the inspector concluded.

'You're not going to find him so easily,' said the baron.

'Why not?'

'Because I never would have thought Nenè capable of murder. If he did it, it means he's lost his head. And it's not easy to know the reasoning of somebody who's lost his head. Whereas you, dear inspector, have a reasoning mind. In short, you're on two different roads that are unlikely to meet.'

✼

'Ntontò opened the door but did not enter the small sitting room where Fofò La Matina was waiting for her. 'What do you want?' she asked from the doorway.

This took Fofò by surprise. Then he noticed that the marchesina was very pale and red-eyed. She was standing quite erect, unnaturally so.

'Come, Marchesa. Please sit down. I have something to tell you.'

'I already know what you have to tell me. I found out two hours ago. From Peppinella, who broke down when I started questioning her. Could you do me a favour?'

'Whatever you like.'

'Settle matters with Papìa, then take care of everything yourself.'

Seven

Taking care of everything was not an easy matter for Fofò. The first hitch came from the fact that Harriet was Protestant.

'What was she protesting about?' said Father Macaluso. 'All she had to do was drop in to the church and everything could have been resolved.'

Another problem was finding Petru's surname and date of birth. That Nettie was Christian, on the other hand, there was no doubt: every morning, when the sun was still rising from the sea, she would open her great window and start singing her praises to the Lord, clapping her hands and shaking all over. It was quite a spectacle. Fofò put the house with the columns up for sale, then gathered together all the documents and papers of Don Totò and his wife to send to America. He also wrote to their children to tell them about the money the marquis had in Vigàta and almost surely in Palermo as well. Only one thing did he put in his own pocket: a little black book in which Don Totò jotted down his daily expenses. The last line of the book said: 'Given to Nenè Impiduglia,' followed by a large sum.

Some ten days later, the inspector headed off on horseback to Misilmeri, a town near Palermo. He had received a letter from a colleague there, and he wanted to verify its contents in person.

As soon as he returned to Vigàta, he summoned Baron Uccello, Father Macaluso, and Fofò La Matina to his office.

'Nenè Impiduglia has been located. He was found naked and dead in a thatched hut outside Misilmeri.'

'Why naked?' the priest asked at once.

'I doubt he took his clothes off himself,' said the inspector. 'It was probably some passers-by. They took everything, down to his underwear. It was probably people who needed clothing.'

'Why dead?' the baron asked, more to the point.

'It's not clear. There were no wounds on the body, except for a few dog bites.'

'I think I know how he died,' Fofò La Matina cut in. 'Did they find a little box beside him?'

'They didn't find anything at all. Only a torn envelope with his name and address on it. Why, what would have been in the box?'

'Insulin and strychnine,' said the pharmacist.

'Good God!' said the inspector.

'I gave them to him myself – the strychnine pills, that is. They were for treating his diabetes, together with the insulin. Did you know he was unwell?'

'No,' the inspector and baron said in a single voice.

'Being a diabetic,' Fofò La Matina continued, 'he must have started feeling ill along the way. Maybe he ran out of pills and was unable to find help.'

'Of course he ran out of pills!' exclaimed Baron Uccello. 'He had used them to poison Don Totò and his family!'

'I don't think so, Baron, not with strychnine.'

'And why not?'

'Because death from strychnine is visible. People's faces and bodies become contorted from the spasms. Whereas at Don Totò's house, everyone was in a natural pose. No, I think that son of a bitch poisoned them with belladonna.'

It was well known that the pharmacist never used profanity, and thus calling Nenè Impiduglia a son of a bitch was out of character for him.

'I'm sorry,' the pharmacist said, taking the little black book out of his pocket and handing it to the inspector. 'Look at the last line. The scoundrel first took the money from Don Totò, and then he killed him.'

'Would you be so kind as to break the news to

'Ntontò, as usual?' the baron asked the pharmacist after a pause.

Fofò remained silent for a moment; it was clear he was weighing the pros and cons.

'No, I won't tell her. Let's let her believe that Impiduglia escaped. I don't know how she would take the news of another death. Her nerves are barely holding up.'

'He can just as well not tell the marchesina about this last death. And he's right not to tell her,' said Colajanni the postmaster later at the club. 'But the fact remains.'

'I don't see what you're trying to insinuate,' said Baron Uccello, defensively. He was very familiar with that tone of voice from Colajanni.

'I'm not trying to insinuate anything. I'm only counting.'

'And what the hell are you counting?'

Colajanni raised the thumb on his right hand and began. 'Don Federico, Rico, Donna Matilde, Don Filippo, Don Totò, Harriet, Petru, Nettie, and Nenè Impiduglia.' When he had finished his list, only the little finger on his left hand was not raised.

'That makes nine,' he continued. 'Have I made myself clear?'

'No, sir, you have not. You must say it in plain speech.'

'What plainer speech is there than this? I am saying the marchesina is doing more damage than an earthquake.'

If Lieutenant Baldovino had not promptly restrained

him, the baron would have pummelled the postmaster's face with his fists.

But the rumour was cast abroad and began to spread quickly through the town because, as we know, slander travels light as a breeze. 'Ntontò, for her part, only stirred the winds up further. Prey to insomnia, she would spend the night walking from room to room with a candle in her hand, and since she also suffered from hot flashes, she was forced to keep the windows open. And so the Vigatese who went to bed late and those who got up early saw her going through her rigmarole and got scared.

'She's always got a tear-soaked handkerchief over her mouth,' said one.

'And her eyes look too wild,' said another.

'I heard her laughing one night,' said a third.

'It was hysteria, I'm sure, but it still makes your hair stand on end.'

The members of the Agrò family discovered by chance, but to their great horror, that they were tenth cousins of 'Ntontò Peluso. Since they didn't know how to read or write, they hired an old crone who in matters of exorcism was the best for miles around.

Shortly thereafter, the pharmacist found an enormous red horn in front of the door to his house, with a note saying: 'For when you go visit the marchesa.'

Opening the door of the palazzo one morning, Mimì

found two live cockerels hanging from one of the handles. He waited a while for someone to come and take them back, and then, when nobody came, he untied them, broke their necks, and made a broth out of them. He didn't know that the cockerels had been purposely put there by Saro Miccichè, whose three-year-old boy was gravely ill. The doctors, even those from Palermo, had examined and prodded him and prescribed remedies, but it was clear they had little hope.

One week after Saro Miccichè had hung the cockerels from the palazzo door, something serious happened: the little boy recovered. And two days later he was running up and down the streets.

Thereafter, not a morning went by without Mimì finding, upon opening up the palazzo, piles of wheat bread, vegetables, quarters of lamb, whole rounds of tumazzo cheese, sausages, baskets of ricotta, cassatas, cannoli, and so on.

'She should thank God we no longer live in times of consequence,' said the postmaster. 'Otherwise, not even the Holy Spirit could have saved 'Ntontò from the stake.'

Then the matter began to die down as it had begun; first of all, because people realized that, despite the offerings made to the marchesa, whoever was supposed to die, died, and whoever was supposed to live, lived; and second, because on certain mornings the bearers of gifts found themselves face to face with Baron Uccello, who would start yelling and slapping and kicking them.

Then 'Ntontò herself removed the burden she had placed on her own shoulders. One Sunday morning, around nine o'clock, she came out of the door and headed to the church in the company of Peppinella. She was still dressed in black, of course, but did not do anything strange; she walked properly and responded with a nod to those who greeted her.

Someone even saw her attempt to smile behind her veil. Then she knelt down in the confessional, took Communion, and returned to the palazzo. That night the windows remained closed.

Another person, however, was seen walking along the beach late into the night, despite a strong north wind, and that person was Father Macaluso. Apparently something was not right with him, since he was talking to himself and gesticulating.

'I want to confess.'

'Have you offended the Lord in word or deed?'

'Yes. I was rude to my servant Mimì and lost my patience with the maid, Peppinella.'

'Those are venial sins, but sins nonetheless. You must be more careful, Marchesa. Five Hail Marys and five Our Fathers. *Ego te*—' He had raised a hand in benediction, knowing from experience that these were the worst of the girl's offences. But 'Ntontò's voice froze him in mid-sentence.

'There's something else.'

'Tell me.'

'When I go to bed at night, I touch myself,' the marchesina said in a different voice, deep and husky.

'What do you mean, you touch yourself?'

'I mean, I touch myself.'

'Where?'

'In the front and in the back, on top and on the bottom. And afterwards I have a good sleep. Till morning.'

'And is that why you do it, to fall asleep?'

'Also.'

'But, Jesus Christ, you can't use a sin as if it was a pill!'

'What can I do, if it makes me feel better? And it even gives me pleasure.'

'Do you touch yourself only once?'

'No, some nights many times.'

'Many?'

'Many.'

'And do you do these things only to help yourself fall asleep, or are you thinking of someone in particular?'

'I'm thinking of someone.'

'Who?'

'I'm ashamed to tell you.'

'You must tell me, otherwise I can't give you absolution.'

'I think of Fofò La Matina.'

This was what Father Macaluso was repeating to himself as he walked along the beach. And it gave him no peace.

'Ntontò's conscience had always been like a great white sheet of paper; now it was stained with a nasty blot of black ink.

'I want to confess.'

'In the name of the Father, the Son, and the Holy Spirit. Speak, Marchesa.'

'The day before yesterday I slapped Peppinella after she talked back to me.'

'Marchesa, for the love of God, you can skip the crap. Let's get to the point. Still?'

'Yes.'

'Every night?'

'Yes.'

'And on certain nights, several times in a row?'

'Yes.'

'And are you still thinking of the same man?'

'Yes.'

'I was expecting this, Marchesa. Over the past week I've thought things over. It is my duty to save your soul. You realize that, don't you?'

'Yes.'

'Well, I have an idea. Listen carefully.'

'Yes.'

'Would you take the pharmacist for your husband?'

'Yes.'

Fofò La Matina had just sat down to eat when he heard knocking at the door and a voice cursing outside. He descended the wooden staircase, opened the door, and was immediately seized by the collar and thrust up against a bench. Father Macaluso was in a rage.

'Pig! Scoundrel! How dare you appear in a young girl's fantasies! You should be ashamed of yourself!'

'What for?' the pharmacist managed to say, half asphyxiated.

'Ah, the innocent man doesn't know!'

'I swear I don't.'

'Well, if you don't know, I'm not going to tell you. But you shall do what I say, or I'll break you in two, so help me God!'

'And would you like to tell me what it is I'm supposed to do?'

'You must marry Marchesina 'Ntontò,' Father Macaluso shot out, finally letting go of Fofò's neck.

The pharmacist froze. 'Are you joking?'

'No, I am not.'

'Look at me: the marchesina is descended from Frederick II, whereas I have only just descended from the tree I used to pick the fruit from and sell it.'

'It doesn't matter.'

'What do you mean, it doesn't matter? The only condition set by Don Filippo and Don Totò was that her fiancé must be noble.'

'And how the bloody hell do you think they're going to object? Haven't you noticed that there isn't a living soul left around 'Ntontò?'

'So whom should I ask for her hand?'

''Ntontò herself. And today.'

'But does the marchesa want me?'

'She wants you, she wants you. Christ, does she want you!'

'Let's go upstairs and talk this over calmly.'

They talked about it for another two hours. Fofò had lost his appetite, but apparently it had been transferred to the priest, who polished off all the food on the table as he was knocking down one after another of the pharmacist's observations.

'But when would this marriage take place?' asked Fofò, expressing his last doubt.

'What do you mean, when? In a month.'

'What about the dispensation from mourning?'

'That's already been taken care of. The bishop ate up a small fortune to clear the way for Impiduglia.'

It was pointless to resist. And so, at nightfall, dressed in a clean suit, with Father Macaluso at his side, the pharmacist showed up at the palazzo. 'Ntontò was waiting for him in the sitting room. Saying nothing, she merely gestured to Fofò to sit down beside her on the sofa, and for the priest to sit in an armchair. Then, as though summoned by her eyes, the pharmacist, who had kept his head turned towards a painting, began to turn around. And at last they looked each other in the eye.

When they returned from their honeymoon – a fortnight in Palermo, at the Hotel des Palmes – Fofò and 'Ntontò were transformed.

'Ntontò looked ten years younger; she had become a young girl again, always laughing, appearing in a different dress every Sunday. She had put the years of mourning and tears behind her. Fofò La Matina, on the other hand, became more gloomy and taciturn with each passing day. Sometimes he didn't respond when greeted, spent all day holed up in the pharmacy, and in the evening, before going home to the palazzo, he would take a long, solitary walk along the water's edge, watching the crabs as they walked beside him. He had never had any friends, and didn't make any new ones, either.

'The compresses you gave me to put on my eyes have done me a world of good,' said Baron Uccello. 'Could you prepare some more for me?'

'Certainly,' said the pharmacist. He went into the back

room and returned with a small glass jar full of black powder. 'This is all I have left,' he said. 'But tomorrow's Sunday, so I'll go to La Mantellina to gather some more.'

'You're going to La Mantellina?'

'Yes, there's a rocky spur there that's full of this plant.'

'Take a rifle.'

'Why?'

'Because I was told that just a day or two ago, around La Mantellina, a peasant was bitten by a rabid dog and died.'

Fofò decided to take the baron's advice. When he reached the rocky spur, a desolate site whose sole vegetation consisted of melilot, the grass he was interested in, and stalks of sorghum, he realized — or perhaps it was the rifle strapped to his shoulder that made him realize — that the place was full of hares and rabbits. He killed two hares and one rabbit, then stopped shooting, since he had nowhere to put any more animals.

This was how he developed a mania for hunting. Unsatisfied with the rifles he found in the palazzo, he went to Palermo and bought himself four that were a pure delight. Three months later, two English bloodhounds arrived, a breed that could smell their quarry from a mile away. Little by little, Fofò was seen less and less about town. He had turned the pharmacy over to an assistant about whom nobody had any complaint.

*

Promoted to the rank of captain, Lieutenant Baldovino had to leave Vigàta, and the town's garrison was sent a new commander: Lieutenant Emiliano di Saint Vincent, a Piedmontese nobleman from Asti. At the club, a party was held to say goodbye to the departing Baldovino and to welcome the new arrival; there were many toasts and much emotion, because Baldovino, after all these years, was considered one of the town.

'But he's an angel!' said Signora Clelia, as soon as she saw Lieutenant Emiliano.

Tall, blond, and quite elegant, Emiliano di Saint Vincent, throughout the reception, spoke, saluted, clicked his heels, and bowed, but did it all as if he were somewhere else. He seemed distant, unreachable.

'When will I ever get my hands on this one?' wondered Signora Clelia, a bit discouraged.

In fact, Lieutenant Emiliano politely declined the generous solicitations of Signora Clelia, who had wanted him to rent the little flat across the landing from hers, the very same that Nenè Impiduglia had inhabited.

'I prefer to sleep at the barracks, with my men.'

'But it's uncomfortable in the barracks!'

'We are soldiers, signora; we are used to discomfort.' And not only was he quite at home with discomfort; he felt it was his duty to make his men live with it as well. When Amedeo Baldovino was in charge, their quarters had become a sort of little town apart, but one which enjoyed all the liberties of the town itself. Reveille was sounded quite a bit later on cold and rainy days, and the soldiers returned to barracks at whatever hour of the night they pleased. With Emiliano di Saint Vincent, however, hours became regular again, with drills in the courtyard early each morning, and the scourge of long marches through the countryside. The few times he was seen in town, the lieutenant never made small talk with anyone, never once eyed a woman, and was uninterested in joining the club.

'Bloodhounds!'

The voice behind him caught Fofò La Matina by surprise as he was stepping out of the door of the palazzo with his two dogs to go hunting. Turning around, he saw a beautiful young man in uniform. He immediately realized this must be the new garrison commander, whom he had not yet met.

'I am Emiliano di Saint Vincent, the new—'

'Yes, I guessed as much. My name is Fofò La Matina; I am the town pharmacist.'

'May I?' the lieutenant asked, and, without waiting for an answer, he crouched down. At once the two dogs started regaling him. The officer patted them, looked inside their mouths, patted them again, then stood up again.

'My compliments,' he said. 'They are two fine specimens, very well taken care of.'

'Do you know about these things?'

'I've got two myself, at home in Asti. And I've also got two foxhounds.'

'But they're for fox hunting.'

'Right. But they're very fast. And speed is always useful, in any hunting dog.'

Fofò realized that it had been months since he'd had so long a conversation with another person.

'Would you like to come hunting with me?'

He had never invited anyone to keep him company.

'Thank you. I would be delighted to come. But I haven't got any of my rifles here.'

'I'll lend you one of mine. Follow me.'

He took him to the flat he had above the pharmacy, which he had turned into an arsenal. It had all of the Pelusos' rifles as well as the four very modern ones he had bought in Palermo. There was also a large table with boxes of gunpowder, scales, measuring cups, empty cartridges, loaded cartridges, caps, crimpers, scoops, fuses, and cartridge belts. Emiliano di Saint Vincent felt almost moved.

'I've got a room just like this, at home in Asti.'

They started talking about gunpowders and rifles. And Fofò was quick to answer. And every so often when they came to a pause, they looked each other in the eye and smiled.

Eight

The two men got into the habit of going hunting together two or three times a week, when the lieutenant could free himself from his military duties. In the meantime Emiliano di Saint Vincent had escaped to Palermo to buy two new rifles, since he did not want to take advantage of his friend's kindness and because, like any good hunter, he wanted his weapons to adapt to his body like a suit that has been well worn in. But these days of hunting were eating away at the pharmacist. For all the attention and concentration he put into his shooting, the lieutenant was always quicker and more accurate. He aimed and squeezed the trigger with elegance; it all looked so effortless, and yet the partridge and quail, rabbits and hares were always cut down in their tracks. Fofò couldn't keep up with him.

'You hardly seem to take aim, Lieutenant.'

'Well, in fact, I don't aim the same way as you. I point the rifle not at the animal, but at the impression I have of it.'

One day, as they were resting from a long outing, Emiliano di Saint Vincent said to the pharmacist: 'You know what? Tomorrow is my birthday.'

'Come and celebrate it at my house,' Fofò replied cheerfully.

Happy to see a new face, 'Ntontò had Peppinella prepare a dinner to remember. And the lieutenant did justice to each course, without once holding back. It was clear that 'Ntontò and the lieutenant had taken a liking to each other; they talked and laughed so much between them that at one point Fofò felt it might be better if he got up and went to bed. There was, moreover, a curious resemblance between the two; they looked like brother and sister, both tall and blond and blue-eyed. And it also seemed as if they had known each other for a long time. Thus lulled by their intense conversation, Fofò began to feel sleepy and finally succumbed in front of a glass of wine. He woke up again as St Vincent was saying goodbye.

'Are we going hunting tomorrow?' he asked the lieutenant.

'No, tomorrow I can't. But the day after tomorrow, with pleasure.'

They made an appointment.

To repay in some way the exquisite hospitality of the marchesa and the pharmacist, the Piedmontese officer decided to uphold a tradition of his people and show his courtesy by missing an easy shot. This allowed Fofò, who was hot on the trail of a partridge, to catch up with him at last. And clearly the contentment he felt from this parity, which he had never before achieved on any of their hunting parties, guided his hand and eye from that moment on; indeed, over the next few hours he gained such an advantage that there was no way the lieutenant would ever surpass him.

They became so dogged in their pursuit of prey that they kept on shooting straight through lunchtime; not until around five o'clock in the afternoon, when they were so tired they could barely stand up, did they decide to take a break. With his back against a tree trunk, a flask of wine between his legs, his dogs lying at his side, his friend sitting beside him, and the fresh smell of grass all around, Fofò La Matina began to enjoy a sensation he had never experienced before in his life. He felt weightless, so much so that he was afraid a slightly stronger gust of wind might lift him to the treetops and higher still, losing him amid the clouds. His chest opened up, and with each breath he felt as if he was taking in two wineskins-full of air. He lost himself staring at an ant that was walking on his hand, watching the effort it made in moving from one hair to another.

'. . . and so we find ourselves in the face of an unusual geometrical progression,' the lieutenant concluded.

Fofò roused himself. He had not heard anything his friend had said. He looked at him.

'I'm sorry,' he said, 'I didn't hear what you were saying.'

The lieutenant looked him in the eye and grew worried. 'What's wrong? Are you unwell?' he asked, putting an arm around Fofò's shoulders. He didn't know that those drawn features, that grimacing mouth were, for Fofò, an expression of happiness.

'No, I feel perfectly fine. What were you saying?'

'I was saying that when the marchesa, your wife, told me about the mournful events of her life, apparently she hadn't noticed. And neither had you, I imagine.'

'But what should I have noticed?'

'The geometric progression. For example: Let us call X the date of the marchesa's grandfather's death or suicide. Four months later, her brother dies, poisoned by mushrooms. Eight months later, her mother dies of a broken heart. Sixteen months later her father, the marquis, meets his maker. Thirty-two months later, her uncle, aunt, and their maid and secretary expire. On nearly the same day as her betrothed. The progression is thus two, four, eight, sixteen, thirty-two. But it is acephalous.'

'Excuse me?'

'It has no beginning. And to find this beginning, we must solve the problem of X minus two. I thought about this all day yesterday, you know. When I was at the barracks. In other words: what happened on the first of

January — that is, two months before the elder marquis killed himself?'

'Ah, well, if that's the problem, it's easily solved,' said Fofò La Matina. 'That's the day I arrived in Vigàta, after having been away for many years.'

'But what have you got to do with any of this?' said the lieutenant, bewildered. 'I don't see the connection.'

'Let me show you. Actually, I had never noticed this business of the numbers. But first I want to tell you the story of a little boy not yet ten years old, the son of a *viddano* — I'm sorry, a peasant — who, though he knew how to gather herbs and roots that could cure every ill, still remained a peasant. This little boy, every time he came into town to deliver things for his father, would walk from street to street with his head tilted back to look up at the little girls on their balconies. One day he looks up at a balcony where he sees a little girl of about six, who happens to belong to the noblest, richest family in town. Their eyes meet and fuse; the boy stands paralysed in the middle of the street, the girl remains motionless, frozen in the act of adjusting a braid. And in the minute that follows, the two grow up and are able to talk to one another with their eyes, like two adults. They keep staring at each other for another two minutes, and in this short span of time they get to know each other, decide they are made for each other, get married, and grow old together. They make an agreement. And when each breaks free of the other's gaze, it becomes a solemn promise. Then the little girl's father arrives and kicks the little boy in the arse, making him drop all the things he was carrying. Would you like to hear a love story that begins this way?'

'Yes. It's a beautiful story,' said the lieutenant, who was a distant relative of Vittorio Alfieri and had a natural bent for such things.

Fofò La Matina leaned more comfortably against his friend's arm, took the lieutenant's hand, which had been resting on his shoulder, into his own, and, borne up by a wave of happiness that very nearly made him sing, he began his tale.

When he finished talking, it was already getting dark. During the telling, Emiliano di Saint Vincent had grown more and more restless and pale. Now, in the darkness, his face shone white. As Fofò uttered his last word, the lieutenant heaved a deep sigh.

'Jesus Christ!' he said, and drank down the last of the wine.

Then he shot out:

'But why did you want to tell me this story? Nobody suspected anything, nobody had connected you in any way with those deaths! Why did you confess to me?'

'Because today I realized I was fed up. For so many years, I obstinately wanted something, and when I finally got it, I realized that it wasn't worth all the trouble.'

'But what are you saying?!'

'Exactly what I said: It wasn't worth the trouble. Not for 'Ntontò, nor for any other girl in the world. I realized this the morning after our wedding night. As she was sleeping there beside me, I looked at her and asked myself: was it worth it?' He paused and extracted a last drop of wine from the flask.

'And you want to know something?' he continued.

'Well, at this point . . .' said the lieutenant, resigned.

'A woman is a poor substitute for a good wank.'

So saying, Fofò didn't realize he was expressing a thought that would occur, many years later, in the same form, to an Austrian named Karl Kraus.

'I don't agree,' said Emiliano di Saint Vincent, attempting to stand up but falling back two or three times to a seating position, his legs as wobbly as a puppet without strings. He made a gesture of despair and said: 'Do you realize that I must do my duty now?'

'Then do it. You'll be acting as a friend, as I have done by telling you the truth.'

And since the other still couldn't manage to stand up, Fofò gave him a hand.

During questioning, he answered: 'The name of Santo Alfonso de' Liguori I chose as a precaution. Returning to Vigàta almost twenty years after my father was murdered, I didn't know if those who had slit his throat and come looking for me were still around. Then Mr Bastiano Taormina explained to me that the people who killed him were monks from elsewhere who thought my father had made a pact with the devil. In Palermo I used to live in the house of an uncle of mine who was a priest and devotee of Santo Alfonso de' Liguori.

'No, I returned to Vigàta only because I wanted to see 'Ntontò again, to see how she had grown up, what she had become. I had no intention to harm anyone. And I was well aware that there was no way I could ever marry her. The Pelusos would never have let me have her; they would never have given their daughter to a peasant's son. It was only when I was sailing on the *Franceschiello* that the thought of killing all the Pelusos occurred to me; but I never imagined I would be capable of carrying it out.

'I never threatened the old marquis. It was he himself, and I don't know how, who realized I had this idea inside me. It was buried deep down, but it was there. And so he threw himself into the sea to avoid being killed by me. But it was this very event that reinforced my idea that if all the Pelusos disappeared, there would be nobody left to oppose our marriage.

'I was called to Rico Peluso's bedside as he was dying. I immediately noticed that his right hand was covered not only with scratches from brambles, there was also the typical triangle left behind by a viper's bite. I simply let

Dr Smecca give him antidotes to mushroom poisoning, but not to viper's venom. Nothing more.

'Donna Matilde would have died anyway, since she refused to go on living. The powders I dissolved in water for her consisted of pulverized valerian, which suppresses hunger. But I doubt she would have ever recovered her appetite, anyway.

'The marquis I killed myself. In the little box of pills I gave him for his stomach acidity I included one of belladonna. But I granted him the time to find happiness and have the baby boy he wanted. That is why I didn't kill him sooner; I liked him, even though he maintained that his daughter's bridegroom had to be a nobleman.

'Nettie the maid used to come to the pharmacy to ask me for the strangest things. One day I sold her some poison, telling her it was a special seasoning for spaghetti. It swept away the lot of them.

'No, the strychnine pills I prepared for Impiduglia were the right medicine. What need would I have had to kill him? In the best of cases, he would have been found guilty of four counts of murder and spent the rest of his life in jail. And 'Ntontò would have forgotten about him. No, I think he died of a diabetic coma.

'The reason I am telling you everything I did is of no interest to anyone. In any case, my wife the marchesa has never known anything about any of this.'

*

'How the hell can he claim that 'Ntontò never knew anything about it?' Father Macaluso burst out. 'After every other Peluso had been wiped off the face of the earth, she came to confession only to convince me that her soul would be forever damned if she couldn't have the pharmacist. She took me for a ride and screwed the holy sacrament of confession into the bargain. The timing was perfect. But knowing the right moment, and choosing the right means, could only be the result of an understanding between the two.'

'But, Father, what are you going to do, report to the inspector what she told you in the confessional?' asked Mrs Colajanni.

'Yeah, you're right, I can't. But it's eating away at me.'

'I'm not so sure there was an agreement between the two,' said Signora Clelia, recalling the day the pharmacist had cleaned her clock inside and out. 'With a love so powerful as the pharmacist's, it's possible 'Ntontò felt it from afar. What do we know about the powers that man has?'

'We would have to ask 'Ntontò,' concluded Mrs Colajanni.

But it wasn't possible to ask 'Ntontò. When Baron Uccello, to whom fell the task of telling the marchesa everything that had happened, had finished speaking, his moustache and beard wet as pastina in a soup of tears,

'Ntontò did not open her mouth except to say: 'Thank you for taking the trouble, Zizì.'

Cool as a cucumber, she sat down at the table at noon on the dot and drank her broth directly from the bowl, without using the spoon, getting it all over her dress.

Later Peppinella, who didn't let her out of her sight, found her playing with two little balls of crumpled paper, lying face down on the floor. The following day, whining and stamping her feet, and stammering in a faint, high-pitched voice, she let Peppinella and Mimì know that she wanted the attic opened up. Finding her little child-hood bed up there, she lay down in it, wet herself, and fell asleep sucking her finger. Summoned by Peppinella, Baron Uccello went to talk to her. Upon seeing him, however, 'Ntontò ran and hid behind a trunk, screaming that she didn't want any doctor and that she didn't have any boo-boos. The baron tried to make her recognize him, but it was no use. Then, bewildered, he asked Peppinella for a glass of water, and the servant went downstairs to fetch one. At that moment, 'Ntontò came out from behind the trunk and looked at him hard and straight in the eye. And the baron, returning her gaze for what seemed an eternity, discovered that there was no madness in those eyes, no return to childhood. They were the eyes of a woman almost thirty years old, full of suffering and awareness. He shuddered.

'What a hideous story, eh, Zizì?'

But when Peppinella returned, she crouched back down behind the trunk. Then something which was not a doubt, but an icy blade — because there could be no more doubt after that look and those words — sliced through the baron's brain, leaving a wound that he would carry with him for the rest of his days.

In vain the defence counsel climbed the slippery slope against all odds. In the face of Fofò's full confession and lack of remorse, the sentence could only have been what it was.

'Now we'll put in an appeal,' said the lawyer.

'No,' said the pharmacist, decisively.

'So, by putting up no opposition, he sent all the lieutenant's numbers to hell,' said Colajanni the postmaster. 'According to those calculations, Fofò should have croaked sixty-four months after the death of Totò Peluso and company.'

'When is the execution to take place?' asked Fede the surveyor.

'In one week.'

'So it adds up. The lieutenant is right. He will die exactly ten months after he was arrested.'

'Would you please explain?'

'Certainly. It only means the numbers decided to change direction and take a different path. Sixty-four months, you say? This time, it's a simple question of addition: six plus four equals ten.'

The firing squad lined up in formation, the first row on one knee, the second one standing. Emiliano di Saint Vincent approached the condemned man, a black cloth in his hand. As he blindfolded him, he whispered, his voice cracking: 'I am truly sorry.'

'I, truly, am not,' said Fofò La Matina.

Author's Note

There is a famous British film about a man, a member of the cadet branch of a noble family, who gets it into his head that he must at all costs become the bearer of the title. And thus, with a little help from chance and a little help from his own brilliance and a rich variety of weapons, he sets about eliminating every one of the successors to the title who stand in his way.

Keeping the family tree always at hand, to remind him of the tasks already accomplished and the challenges that still await, he manages, with a stubbornness typical of saints and scientists, to climb branch after branch like a monkey, until at last he can sit at the top. But a careless mistake, in the end, does him in.

Those who might think my novel grew out of this film would, however, be wrong. The idea for the book came to me twenty-two years ago when reading the two volumes of the historic study *Report on the Social and Economic Conditions of Sicily (1875–1876)*, reprinted by Cappelli Publishers in 1968. Hidden in the one thousand four hundred and forty-eight pages (I say 'hidden' because I no longer feel like finding the exact place) of this study, there is a two-line dialogue between one of the members of the research committee and a representative of the law in a small town:

'Have there recently been any violent crimes in your town?'

'No, with the exception of a pharmacist who killed seven people for love.'

And there you have it. From that moment on, I began to think about this story. And when, together with my friends Suriano and Passalacqua, I scripted a very short story by Leonardo Sciascia for television, titled 'Western about Things of Ours' (*Western di Cose Nostre*), with a heavy heart I gave the protagonist, a pharmacist, a number of the traits of 'my' pharmacist.

It seems to me truly a waste of breath to declare, as I must, that the names and situations presented here are in no way related to real people or real events, aside from the story at the origin of the tale. They are, instead, related to me and my memory of my land.

This novel is dedicated to Rosetta, my wife. I don't think she likes it much; not because of the way it's written, but because of what it means. If so, may she accept this dedication as a new tribute to her more than thirty years of patience in my regard.

[1990]

Notes

page 5 – **Madonna biniditta**: A Sicilian expression of surprise, shock, or alarm, equivalent to something like 'Oh my God!' in English. Literally, it means Blessed Madonna!

page 21 – **. . . the horns on his head were so tall that they could have been used as lighthouses**: In Italian, the fact of having or wearing horns means that one is a *cornuto* – that is, a cuckold.

page 23 – **Marchesina 'Ntontò . . . Marchesino Rico**: The Italian nobility has the custom of calling the offspring of a titled parent by the diminutive of that same title. Thus the son of a *marchese* (Eng. marquess, Fr. *marquis*) is a *marchesino*, the daughter of a *contessa* is a *contessina*, and so on.

page 32 – **'A ricò! Cu a voli a ricò!'**: Sicilian dialect. Literally: 'Ricotta! Who wants ricotta?'

page 41 – **field watcher**: In Sicily, major landowners often resorted to the use of private guards, called *campieri*, to protect their lands and crops from bandits.

page 47 – 'The cuckolded bastard,' . . . 'Do you mean that in a manner of speaking, or is it true?': In Italy, especially Southern Italy, the word *cornuto* ('cuckold'; see note to p. 21, above) is a common insult that doesn't necessarily imply that its target is actually a cuckold.

page 56 – **Sicilian nobles customarily signed with an X. [. . .] Reading and writing were for miserable paper-pushers and clerks:** By the nineteenth century a fair part of the Italian nobility, particularly in the South, was uncultured. One may recall that Fabrizio del Dongo, the young aristocratic protagonist of Stendahl's novel *The Charterhouse of Parma*, was similarly uneducated, though from the north of the peninsula.

page 71 – **They were playing briscola:** An Italian card game.

page 84 – *Fùttiri addritta e camminari na rina, portanu l'omu a la rovina*: 'Fucking while standing and walking on sand will lead a man to his ruin' (Sicilian proverb).

page 98 – **The marquis touched his balls dramatically:** A superstitious gesture for warding off bad luck.

pages 169–70 – . . . **the Piedmontese officer decided to uphold a tradition of his people and show his courtesy:** There is an Italian saying that the '*piemontese è falso e cortese*'; that is, 'the Piedmontese is false and courteous.' Thus the young lieutenant shows his courtesy here by being false – i.e., pretending to miss his quarry.

page 173 – . . . **a distant relative of Vittorio Alfieri and had a natural bent for such things:** Like Emiliano di Saint Vincent, Vittorio Alfieri (1749–1803), the famous poet and dramatist considered the 'father of Italian tragedy', was a Piedmontese nobleman from Asti. His life and work were full of troubled love affairs, usually involving the nobility.

page 181 – **There is a famous British film about a man, a member of the cadet branch of a noble family, who gets it in his head that he must, at all costs, become the bearer of the title:** A reference to *Kind Hearts and Coronets* (1949), directed by Robert Hamer, starring Dennis Price in the central role, and Alec Guinness playing no fewer than eight different roles, including Lady Agatha.

Notes by Stephen Sartarelli